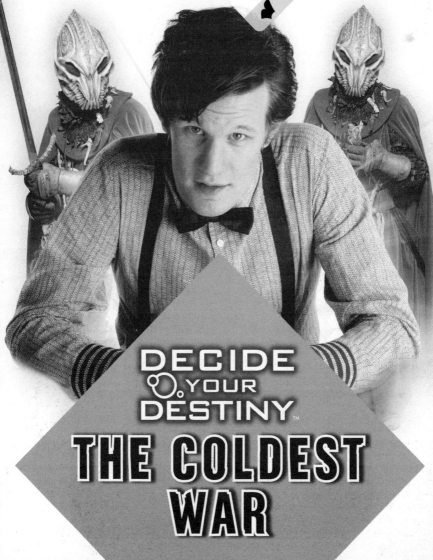

DOCTOR WHO

DECIDE YOUR DESTINY™

THE COLDEST WAR

BBC CHILDREN'S BOOKS
Published by the Penguin Group
Penguin Books Ltd, 80 Strand, London, WC2R 0RL, England
Penguin Group (USA) Inc., 375 Hudson Street, New York 10014, USA
Penguin Books (Australia) Ltd, 250 Camberwell Road, Camberwell, Victoria 3124, Australia
(A division of Pearson Australia Group Pty Ltd)
Canada, India, New Zealand, South Africa
Published by BBC Children's Books, 2010
Text and design © Children's Character Books, 2010
Written by Colin Brake
002
BBC logo © BBC 1996. Doctor Who logo © BBC 2009. TARDIS image © BBC 1963.
Licensed by BBC Worldwide Limited.
BBC, DOCTOR WHO (word marks, logos and devices), and TARDIS are trademarks of the
British Broadcasting Corporation and are used under licence.
ISBN: 978-1-40590-686-9
Printed in Great Britain by Clays Ltd, St Ives plc

www.greenpenguin.co.uk

MIX
Paper from
responsible sources
FSC™ C018179

Penguin Books is committed to a sustainable
future for our business, our readers and our planet.
This book is made from Forest Stewardship
Council™ certified paper.

ALWAYS LEARNING   **PEARSON**

How To Use Your Decide Your Destiny Book

Follow the instructions below before reading this book.

1. Go to: www.doctorwhochildrensbooks.co.uk/decideyourdestiny

2. Click 'Begin' to launch the book selection screen.

3. After selecting your book, the scene selection menu will appear.

4. Start reading the story on page 1 of this book and follow the instructions at the end of each section.

5. When you make a decision that takes you online, select the correct box and enter the corresponding code word as prompted.

6. After watching the scene or completing your online activity, return to the scene selection screen and continue your story.

Now turn the page and begin your adventure!

You stare around at the vast circular room with your mouth hanging open. The space is massive and in the middle is a raised area on which a multi-sided control console occupies the central position.

'You want to close that mouth, you'll catch flies in it,' says the man standing over the controls. The man has a young face and a bush of floppy hair that falls over his features like a curtain, but his eyes are somehow ancient and wise. He wears a slightly old-fashioned tweed jacket and a small bow tie over a plain shirt and dark trousers. When you first saw him you thought he looked like a young university professor. His name is the Doctor.

'Do you get flies in here?' A new voice joins the conversation. This voice is female and has a gently lilting Scottish accent. It belongs to a pretty long-legged girl who is leaning against one of the tall roof supports, watching you and the Doctor with keen and amused eyes.

'Not as a rule, Amy,' the Doctor says, flicking another switch or two on the nearest control panel before stepping towards you with his hand held out. 'But you never know. Do you have that screwdriver then?'

You realise with a start that he is talking to you. The Doctor seems to have a mind that leaps around like a manic bunny rabbit and it's hard to keep up with him.

If you have the screwdriver, go to 45.

If you don't have the screwdriver, go to 81.

'Never!' shouts the Sycorax Warrior. He produces a hand weapon, but instead of aiming at any of you, he fires it up at the ceiling above you. Debris and dust rain down and you throw your arms up to protect yourselves and stagger backwards. When the dust settles you find that the Sycorax Warrior has disappeared.

The Doctor starts pulling the debris out of the way. There is a small mountain of it blocking your path, but with you and Amy helping, you are soon able to clear a passage wide enough to get through.

'We need to get after him,' the Doctor urges you. 'Whatever caused the power drain is in here somewhere and I don't trust our Sycorax friend to treat it very well!'

Moving quickly but carefully, you advance along the corridor. Soon you reach a massive but mostly empty storage chamber. The main feature is a strange crystalline structure that glitters in the middle of the room. It does not look like it belongs here. Standing around the crystal are three humanoid aliens. They have bony ridges on their heads and pale green skin. Each of them has an outstretched hand almost touching the crystal, but they seem to be frozen in time, alive but completely immobile.

The Sycorax Warrior is also there. He, too, is stretching an arm out to touch the crystal.

The Doctor screams out a warning.

If the Sycorax ignores the Doctor, go to 19.

If the Sycorax stops, go to 43.

Speaking through the communications device, the Sycorax answers the Doctor's question.

'We need them to find the Dx87kk=$si2£,' he tells the Doctor.

Amy taps the screen. 'Has this thing stopped working?' she asks.

'That last bit was beyond the translation software,' the Doctor tells you.

'It sounded like Kriftlok,' you say.

The Doctor is nodding. 'I know a little of the Sycorax language — that translates as something like "monster".'

Amy snorts. 'Oh, that's just great. The ugly aliens want human slaves to find something they think is a monster!'

'Release the humans from your control and I will find the Kriftlok,' the Doctor tells the Sycorax, managing to perfectly replicate the guttural pronunciation of the alien word.

The Sycorax does not look very convinced.

'I am a Time Lord of Gallifrey,' announces the Doctor. 'I give monsters nightmares. I can handle this Kriftlok.'

'Whatever it is,' you add, in a whisper.

'The Kriftlok is a mindless beast,' the Sycorax tells you. 'It eats and stores energy like a wild animal eats meat. It is always hungry and it is very dangerous.'

'How come you had it on your ship?' asks Amy.

The Sycorax shrugs. 'There are many who would pay for a galactic curiosity such as the Kriftlok. When we came across one dormant, drifting near a red star, we brought it inside our asteroid.'

'And then... it woke up?' suggests the Doctor.

If the Sycorax continues his story, go to 84.

If something interrupts him, go to 41.

You type in the word SNOWMAN and the screensaver clears to reveal a screen of application icons and shortcuts. The Doctor takes over at the virtual keyboard — a touch-sensitive hologram projection of a QWERTY keyboard on the surface of the desk — and rapidly calls up the personal user log of the computer's operator.

'Right, it's February 24th 2024,' he announces, 'and the base was evacuated two days ago; emergency protocol forty six slash three.'

'And what's that when it's at home?' demands Amy.

'I haven't got a clue,' confesses the Doctor, 'but whatever it was, was serious enough to warrant a full evacuation. Ah!'

'What is it?'

The Doctor spins around in his chair to face you all. 'There's something in Lab 3. It's in complete lockdown and has been since about thirty minutes before the evac.'

'Can't be a coincidence, can it?' says Amy.

The Doctor nods. 'So now we just need to find Lab 3.'

'And get inside it,' adds the Sycorax, fingering his whip, 'but that should prove no problem to me.'

The Doctor eyes the crackling whip nervously. 'Yes, well, hopefully we can find a better way than brute force.'

On the screen he has called up a map of the base. He prods a finger at the image.

'Right, we're here, which means that Lab 3 is right along this corridor.'

He turns around and sees that the Sycorax is already heading out of the door.

'Wait,' he calls.

If the Sycorax Warrior stops, go to 94.

If the Sycorax Warrior ignores him, go to 63.

The Doctor looks more serious than you have ever seen him.

'Dangerous?' he repeats. 'Get this wrong and that's the whole solar system wiped out.'

Before he can explain more, you hear a scream.

Running back out into the larger lab, you find Cathleen being menaced by half a dozen of the zombie-like coma patients. They have her backed into a corner.

'They don't look very strong,' Amy says, with a determined look on her face. 'Can't we just rush them?'

The Doctor shakes his head. 'Someone could get hurt and it could be us.'

To your surprise, he raises his hands and allows the shuffling patients to add the three of you to their cordon. Once you are all trapped together, they stop moving.

'See,' the Doctor tells you, 'they just want to immobilise us.'

'So what happens next?' you ask.

'Wait and see,' says the Doctor, but you see that he is slowly slipping a hand into one of his jacket pockets, ready for something.

There are about six of the zombie patients holding you in the corner of the room. The other six start shuffling towards the glass box in the middle of the floor.

'I thought as much,' says the Doctor and you see that he has now produced his sonic screwdriver.

He quickly points it at the door, fires a blast of sound and the door slides shut with a satisfying CLUNK.

If the zombies use the keypad, go to 44.

If a new figure appears, go to 78.

Amy suddenly spots something on the horizon.

'Look!' she cries, 'What's that?'

You look in the direction that she is pointing, but at first you can't see what it is that has caught her eye. The all-pervading whiteness of the snow makes it hard to see anything, but then you realise what it is that she has seen.

'That lump of snow?'

Amy nods enthusiastically. 'But it's not just a lump of snow, is it? Look at the shape. That's not a natural shape, is it?'

The Doctor is now looking himself, using a pair of binoculars that he has fished from a pocket.

'No, it's not,' he agrees, passing you the glasses so that you can see for yourself.

Through the binoculars you can see for yourself that it isn't just snow.

'It's another spaceship!' you declare.

It's partly covered in snow but there is no mistaking the fact that it is a large metallic object at a slightly odd angle. It looks a bit like a traditional flying saucer with some additional fins.

'Mark Three Hopper, with Trans System Fission Drive,' the Doctor tells you. 'Nice little mover.'

You and Amy just look at him.

'Don't go all *Top Gear* on us,' says Amy, 'you sound like Rory talking about sports cars.'

'Do you think it is another victim of the power drain?' you ask.

'Let's find out,' suggests the Doctor and sets off towards it.

If you find the entrance, go to 51.

If the Doctor finds the entrance, go to 15.

Amy takes a step closer to the container. 'It looks like pink blancmange,' she tells you, reaching out a hand to touch it. 'Oh!'

'What happened?' asks the Doctor, running to join her.

'It moved,' says Amy. She reaches out again and this time the liquid runs over her hand.

'I can hear it,' Amy says, surprised at the sensation. 'Inside my head, I can hear her voice. She's so sad and in such pain.'

The Doctor looks furious. 'Let me talk to her,' he says, pushing his sleeves up before plunging both arms into the liquid.

He throws back his head and closes his eyes as the liquid pours out of the container, up his arms and covers his entire body.

'Doctor!' Amy is worried.

'It didn't hurt you, did it?' you remind her.

A moment later the liquid retreats from the Doctor and spills back into the container. The Doctor shakes his head and runs a hand through his hair.

'Wow!' he says.

'What happened?' asks Amy.

'Communication,' replies the Doctor.

'So what did she say? Was she responsible for draining the TARDIS energy? And the Sycorax ship too?' you ask.

'Yes,' confesses the Doctor, 'yes, she was.'

'Then she must pay,' says a familiar voice. You turn around to see that the Sycorax Warrior has joined you, whip in his hand ready to use.

If the Doctor stops him in time, go to 35.

If the Doctor doesn't reach him in time, go to 67.

The Doctor tries to use the sonic screwdriver to loosen the screws, but without any success.

'It's no good,' he tells you, 'it needs more brute force than the sonic screwdriver can manage.'

You remember that you've still got the screwdriver that you let the Doctor borrow back home in your pocket. You retrieve it and give it to him. 'Would this be better?' you ask him.

'Brilliant!' The Doctor takes the screwdriver from you and, a few moments later, all four screws have been extracted.

'Right, who wants to go first?' the Doctor asks.

You and Amy look into the hole that has been revealed and exchange a glance. There is a narrow steel passageway, tall enough to crawl through, but not large enough to stand in.

'I'll go first,' Amy volunteers. The Doctor helps Amy climb into the hole and then gives you a bunk-up too. Finally he hauls himself into the space.

You crawl along on hands and knees, trying to keep up with Amy, who is already some way ahead of you.

'Don't go too fast,' you call out.

'I just want to get to the other end and get out,' Amy calls back.

You can't blame her. It is very dark and cramped in here and you can feel your heart thumping in your chest as you crawl along as fast as you dare.

Suddenly you reach a T-junction. Looking both ways, you fail to see any sign of Amy.

If you go left, go to 52.

If you go right, go to 54.

'Yes, please,' you tell the Doctor with enthusiasm. 'But where to? If you really can go anywhere in time and space... the choices are endless.'

'Why don't we let the TARDIS decide?' suggests the Doctor.

Without warning he suddenly runs over to the mushroom-shaped console and pushes his jacket sleeves up over his shirt cuffs like a concert pianist about to play. For a moment he hesitates and then, WHOOSH, his hands become a blur as he flicks switches and turns knobs all around the control panels. Finally he stops, gives you a quick grin and then pulls a large lever.

Instantly the sound of ancient and unknowable engines starts up, groaning and screaming like a nightmare zoo. There is almost no sensation of movement at all.

'Shouldn't we sit down and put seat belts on?' you ask, nervously.

The Doctor shakes his head. 'No, no need at all.'

Amy catches your eye. 'It might not be a bad idea to stand near something you can hold on to,' she suggests, 'just in case.'

Without any warning, the floor seems to buckle and you are thrown to the ground. The engine sounds change, becoming agonisingly drawn out. The TARDIS is now shaking like the worst roller coaster ride ever. The Doctor is running around the console operating controls, but with no effect.

Suddenly a deep sonorous bell begins to sound like an alarm.

'What's happening?' you ask.

If Amy answers, go to 59.

If the Doctor answers, go to 66.

'The device in that room is mine,' the Sycorax tells you. 'It was stolen from me by a low-lying thief, a shape-shifting Yarkop.'

The Doctor nods. 'I've met Yarkops. They're sneaky, I'll give you that.'

'The thief stole the device and sought to hide it here, in this pathetic planet.' The human mouthpiece of the alien falls silent for a moment and then continues more hesitantly, 'Sycorax are... forbidden to visit here.'

The Doctor grins and winks at you. 'Guess who's responsible for that!' he whispers.

'So I teleported alone to secure my prize,' the Sycorax explains. 'Let me have it and we will leave this system for good.'

The Doctor nods and slowly bends to pick up his sonic screwdriver.

'That's all very well but that device in there is no more yours than it is the Yarkop's. That's a micro-universe, the sort of thing the WarpWeavers of Blue Halo Alpha knock up.'

The Sycorax and his human voice box remain silent.

'Now the WarpWeavers know what they're doing. You don't,' continues the Doctor.

'I know a powerful energy battery when I see one,' insists the alien.

'You think that's just an energy container?' screams the Doctor.

'It's a pocket universe! When my space-time machine happened to pass in range, it sucked every last atom of power from it. Making it a very unstable micro-universe. One false move and we'll all go up.'

You can see that the Doctor is seriously worried about this.

'You're bluffing,' responds the Sycorax.

Go to 14.

'Tell me more,' the Doctor asks, gently.

The Professor gets to his feet. 'Only if you tell me how you recognised what we are doing here.'

'I've seen the like before,' the Doctor tells the Professor.

'But that's not possible. I invented this technology,' Professor Howkins insists, getting back on his feet.

'On this planet, yes,' agrees the Doctor, 'but it's not unknown elsewhere. Question is, how did you come to it? I seem to recall that it's the twenty-second century before this technology shows up on Earth.'

'Enough of talking,' interrupts the Sycorax. 'We must shut down this machinery now.'

'But that's just it,' insists the Professor. 'I can't.'

He takes a deep breath and begins to explain.

'This whole project was full of dangers. That's why we came here, to the Antarctic, well away from inhabited places, to create the experiments. The extractor is meant to remove potential energy from micro-elements in the atmosphere and convert them into storable forms of energy.'

The Doctor nods. 'But it's gone wrong, hasn't it?'

'There was an overload. Critical systems burnt out, including the safety cut-outs and overrides. Most of my team were killed instantly, vaporised by random energy bolts. And now I can't shut it off. It's sucking in more and more energy, like a bottomless cup.'

'Or a mini black hole,' comments the Doctor, his face serious, 'which is what you've made.'

If the Doctor carries on speaking, go to 71.

If the Sycorax Warrior acts, go to 87.

You lead the way and the lift deposits you in the igloo lobby, where your special arctic wear clothes are waiting for you. Soon you are fully kitted out in the lightweight but warm clothing and ready to step out into the snowy wasteland again. As soon as you exit on to the plains, you see a smoking crater of partially melted snow where the Sycorax ship had crashed.

The Doctor looks up and points at a particular bright star moving across the sky.

'There they go, and good riddance,' he says with feeling. 'Not my favourite aliens,' he tells you, 'cost me a hand first time I met them. Caused no end of trouble that hand...'

Amy is looking around and you can see that she is frowning behind her reflective dark glasses.

'Err Doctor... where's the TARDIS?'

You look around in a complete circle. As far as you can remember, the TARDIS was pretty much directly opposite the door to the igloo, about two hundred metres away from it. However, while you were down below it has snowed again and now there is no sign of the bright blue Police Box at all.

The Doctor tells you not to worry. He pulls off one of his gloves, raises his hand and theatrically clicks his fingers. In response, the

TARDIS suddenly reveals itself with a flash of its lights, as the snow that has been covering it falls away from its sides and one of the doors opens automatically.

'Time to go home,' says the Doctor.

THE END

The Doctor leads you and Amy out into the base. You can't help but be a little disappointed. The Doctor said his machine could take you anywhere in time and space, but instead of an alien vista or a prehistoric panorama you have a plain grey corridor, lit by recessed ceiling lights.

The Doctor locks the TARDIS and takes a deep breath. 'Definitely recycled air,' he tells you.

'I wonder where we are?' Amy wonders.

You walk ahead, hoping to see something more exciting. You come across a door with a red cross sticker on it. Peering through the glass panel set into the door, you see a number of what look like hospital beds.

'Sick bay,' mutters the Doctor, peeking over your shoulder. 'Must be time for the Doctor's round.'

Acting for all the world as if he is meant to be there, the Doctor opens the door and steps inside. You and Amy follow him.

Inside the room you can see that it is set out like a small hospital ward with a dozen beds lined up against the walls. Each of the beds is occupied with a patient but none of them seem to be awake.

'Is this a good idea?' Amy asks, 'They might be contagious.'

The Doctor shakes his head. 'They'd be in isolation if that were the case. I think we're safe.'

If the Doctor starts to examine one of the patients, go to 29.

If the door opens and someone enters, go to 57.

'I am not bluffing,' insists the Doctor. 'Look, that micro-universe runs on enormous amounts of energy. But when it stole the power from my space-time ship it became unstable. Listen to me.'

But the Sycorax is not prepared to listen. Ignoring the Doctor, he crosses to the door of the glass room, punches in the access code and strides inside. Dodging the now motionless zombies, the Doctor, you and Amy hurry after him.

Inside the room, the Sycorax reaches out to grab the fragile-looking soap bubble in the middle of the equipment. You can see vibrations on the surface of the bubble and the milky interior is now flashing with bursts of coloured light.

'No, don't!' screams the Doctor, but it appears that the Sycorax has had enough of listening. His hands reach into the heart of the scaffolding.

Suddenly there is a burst of orange lightning flying across the room from somewhere behind you, which hits the Sycorax squarely on the back of the shoulders. His body arches backwards, lit up from within, and then he crumbles to dust.

The Doctor spins round. 'There was no need for that!' he roars.

You turn too and are shocked to see the focus of his anger.

In the doorway of the glass room stands Trainee Nurse Cathleen, but she no longer looks the friendly, helpful woman that you first met. Her expression is hard and determined and in her hand she holds a futuristic-looking hand blaster.

'Step away,' she orders, tersely.

The Doctor shakes his head. 'I can't do that,' he tells her.

Cathleen begins to vibrate and her features begin to blur. Before your amazed eyes, she starts morphing and changing into something else. In seconds, the human figure is completely gone, to be replaced by an ugly rhino-headed humanoid figure in black leather.

'Perhaps this form will persuade you?' it says, still using Cathleen's voice, which rather detracts from any fear engendered by the transformation.

'A Judoon?' says the Doctor. 'Not gonna scare me with a Judoon.'

The shape-shifting Yarkop shimmers again and this time takes on the form of a reptilian humanoid with a domed forehead.

'A Draconian, very good,' says the Doctor. 'Do you do requests?'

With a roar of fury, the shape-shifter pushes past him and reaches out for the soap bubble. As soon as its fingers make contact there is a flash of intense white light.

'Get down!' screams the Doctor.

You hit the floor and put your hands over your head. You can feel the heat above as energy bolts fill the air. There is a sound like the loudest firework display you have ever seen.

If there is a great big BOOM, go to 75.

If everything goes dark, go to 21.

It doesn't take as long as you had first thought to reach the ship, which is as tall as a house and about four times the length.

The Doctor becomes excited as he gets closer. 'That's interesting,' he mutters to himself, 'not a Mark 3 but a Mark 4 with some retro restyling...'

'Doctor...' Amy says, in a warning tone.

'Sorry,' he tells her. He starts moving around the ship and tells you that 'the main airlock should be along here somewhere...' and then he disappears from view. You and Amy follow him around a corner and find him opening the outer doors of an airlock with the sonic screwdriver. The metallic door rolls up and the three of you are able to enter.

The Doctor hits a control and the door slides shut again. You pull your hood off your head.

'Wow, it's warm in here.'

The Doctor leans across and fiddles with a control on your suit. 'That should be better,' he tells you, 'these suits can keep you cool as well as warm.'

After doing the same for Amy, the Doctor opens the inner door of the airlock. Beyond, there is a small lobby area and two corridors, disappearing in different directions.

'That's weird,' comments Amy.

'What?' you ask her.

'Well, the power's on, isn't it?' You look around and realise that she is right. Lights are on, heating is on. Unlike the TARDIS, this spaceship still seems to have its energy intact.

If you go left, go to 37.

If you go right, go to 77.

The creature, still disguised as a Sycorax, nods its head.

'You will guarantee my freedom?' he asks.

'I promise,' says the Doctor.

'Very well.' The fake Sycorax takes a deep breath and then throws his arms wide and begins to pulsate with blue light. Behind him, the Sycorax engines begin to come alive as power floods back into the energy chambers.

The process takes a few minutes, but finally the light fades and standing where the fake Sycorax had been standing is a small grey humanoid with large blue eyes.

Before anyone can say anything, the Sycorax Leader pushes past the Doctor and launches an attack with the energy whip. For a horrible moment the energy crackles along the whip and dances all over the body of the grey shape-shifter, but then the energy seems to go in reverse, back up the length of the whip before going on to smother the Sycorax. The two aliens are linked in a jittery dance of death and the deadly energy flows back and forth.

Finally there is a loud popping noise and both creatures fall to the floor, smoking like firewood falling from a bonfire.

Amy hurries across to the Sycorax and carefully feels for a pulse. 'It's no good,' she reports, 'he's dead.'

The Doctor, meanwhile, has hurried to the side of the shape-shifter. He shakes his head, sadly. 'This one too,' he reports.

If you go to the Doctor, go to 65.

If Amy goes to the Doctor, go to 76.

The voice is harsh and deep, but its words are clear. 'What have you done to my ship?'

You turn around and see that you are surrounded by about a dozen fierce-looking aliens. They have a humanoid shape but seem to have a partial exo-skeleton, giving them a bony outer skull over exposed muscle. Their eyes burn angry and red. They are dressed in long blood red cloaks decorated with what appears to be hair, dried skin and bones.

'Sycorax,' mutters the Doctor, recognising them. 'You are not meant to be here. This planet is protected.'

The leader of the Sycorax takes a step forward. 'You think we want to be here? We were attacked. Power stolen. We crashed on this miserable rock.'

Amy steps forward bravely. 'Us too,' she tells the alien. 'We're in the same boat.'

'How come they speak English?' you whisper.

'They don't,' the Doctor whispers back, 'The TARDIS is translating for you.'

The Sycorax Leader is considering Amy's words. 'Your ship was also drained of power?' he asks.

The Doctor nods. 'Almost completely. And something out here must be responsible.'

The Sycorax Leader comes to a decision and gestures to his men.

'Wait, where are you going?' the Doctor asks.

'There is a human settlement under the ice,' the alien tells him. 'Something called The Antarctic Research Base. It must be the source of the power drain.'

The Sycorax turns away.

'No, wait.'

If the Sycorax turns back, go to 89.

If the Sycorax leave, go to 96.

You are trapped in the corner of the room. The coma patients, who a moment ago had been as lifeless as shop dummies, are now shuffling towards you, arms outstretched, eyes open but unseeing.

The Doctor turns around and examines the wall closely, his sonic screwdriver in his hands.

'Doctor! Now would be a good time to do something clever,' urges Amy, not taking her eyes off the advancing patients.

'Trying,' says the Doctor, tersely. You can hear the sonic screwdriver whirring and then there is a bang and when you turn around, you see that the Doctor has managed to remove one of the panels that make up the wall of the ward. 'Got to love pre-fab buildings,' he mutters, ushering Cathleen, Amy, and you through the hole in the wall before diving through himself.

'What's going on?' asks Cathleen.

'At a guess, some kind of remote control using blood chemistry,' the Doctor tells her. 'I've seen something like it before.'

The four of you are now running down the corridor.

'What are your people working on here?' asks the Doctor.

'That's classified information,' Cathleen tells him. 'I don't have security clearance to tell you.'

'Well, who does?' demands Amy.

'Most of the crew are back there.' She waves a hand in the direction of the zombie patients. 'The only other crewmember left is Yasin.'

'And where can we find him?' asks the Doctor.

'With the find, of course.' Cathleen explains that the base was created to allow a team of specialists to investigate something that was found buried in the Antarctic ice. She cannot tell you any more detail but takes you to a lower level, where she says Yasin will be able to help.

You travel in a lift shaft, which takes you to a massive underground chamber that appears to have been cut into rock.

'We had to drill down into this rock,' Cathleen explains, 'but once we were in, we found it full of caves and caverns. Thing is, the geologists can't explain how it came to be here.'

'So, is this it?' you ask. 'Is this rock the mysterious "find"?'

'Oh no,' Cathleen grins and leads you down a passageway cut crudely into the rock.

She takes you to a smaller chamber, which is filled with machinery. There are valves and pipes and wires; it looks like something you'd find in a factory or on an industrial estate. It is certainly the last thing you would expect to find in a cave. The Doctor, however, doesn't look at all surprised.

'Cathleen, who on earth are these people?' A worried-looking young Indian man dressed in plain overalls appears from behind the machinery.

Cathleen introduces you to Yasin. He is the deputy leader of the project.

'Let me guess,' says the Doctor, 'you were a late appointment to the project and never had your blood sample taken?'

'How can you know that?' demands Yasin.

If the Doctor answers, go to 23.
If Amy answers, go to 47.

The Sycorax Warrior ignores the Doctor and touches the crystal. Instantly he screams and tries to pulls his arm away, but a rapid paralysis is gripping his body, starting at his hand.

'No!' he cries, trying to pull his frozen hand away with his free one. But the paralysis is spreading, across his shoulders, down his torso, up on to his face. In seconds he is completely frozen, unable to move, unable to speak.

The Doctor shakes his head sadly. 'I did try and warn him,' he tells you.

'What happened to him?' you ask.

The Doctor indicates the three green-skinned aliens. 'Same thing as happened to this lot,' he tells you, 'they've been frozen in time.'

'How?' asks Amy, 'Is that some kind of time machine?'

The Doctor walks around the crystal, examining it but making sure he keeps clear. 'No, not really. Certainly not by design.'

The Doctor takes a step closer to one of the green-skinned aliens. 'These guys are Atraian Traders. Like the Sycorax, they're a kind of parasite race, using the achievements of others rather than making things themselves. Although at least the Atraians pay their way. But they've had a bit of bad luck here. I doubt they knew what they were buying.'

'This crystal thing?' you ask.

The Doctor nods. 'An H'R'R'luurniki Crystal Energy Convertor — semi-organic technology from the H'R'R'lurrniki Cluster. It's a self-sustaining energy storage system, but it was never designed to absorb time energy like it found on my ship. It's leaking artron energy — that's what's frozen these guys in time.'

'So can you turn it off? Reverse the energy flow?' asks Amy.

'I can't see any controls for it,' you point out.

'There aren't any,' says the Doctor, 'its control systems are all organic. The only way for me to control it is through telepathy.'

'Can you do that?' wonders Amy, with an alarmed look on her face.

'Not with humans, not without a great deal of effort, but with this crystal... hopefully.'

He reaches out a hand towards the crystal.

'But won't you get frozen like this lot?' screams Amy.

'I'm a Time Lord,' he reminds her, 'hopefully I'm time-sensitive enough to overcome it!'

And with that he touches the crystal. Instantly, reality seems to fold in on itself and everything goes black.

When you come round you are surprised to find that you are lying on the snow outside the TARDIS. Amy is lying next to you.

'Are you both okay?' asks the Doctor.

You allow him to help you to your feet.

'What happened?' you ask him.

The Doctor grins. 'It worked. I reversed the energy flow and hit the reset button.'

'What happened to the aliens?' asks Amy, getting up.

'Gone. Both the Sycorax and the Atraians have gone back to their ships and taken off. The base here is safe.'

Amy smiles. 'Shall we pop in and tell them?' she wonders.

The Doctor shakes his head. 'Why bother them? They don't need to know that they were ever in danger. Come on then, back to the TARDIS. Time for you,' he looks at you, 'to go home.'

THE END

You type the numbers 7890 into the keypad and to your surprise, the door springs open.

'It worked!'

You take a step across the threshold and immediately feel yourself being pulled back again. An energy whip flashes across the space you had just occupied and you realise, with horror, that there is a Sycorax Warrior attacking you. The Doctor and Amy pull you to safety, but rather than try again, the Sycorax turns and runs off, his red cloak flying out behind him.

'Come on,' urges the Doctor, 'after him! The Sycorax must have found out what's behind all this.'

The Doctor hurtles after the Sycorax and you and Amy, slightly confused, run after him.

The corridor beyond the bulkhead door leads to another door but this lies broken in two massive pieces that are still smoking from being torn apart.

The Doctor nimbly hurdles over the pieces to enter the room beyond, while you and Amy take a more cautious route around them.

When you join the Doctor inside the room, you find him confronting the Sycorax across a strange crystal structure that dominates the centre of the large chamber. Around the edge of the crystal there are three other aliens, humanoids with strangely ridged heads, pale green skins and outstretched arms. They seem to be frozen like statues.

The Sycorax is reaching out towards the crystal structure.

'Don't touch it!' screams the Doctor.

If the Sycorax ignores the Doctor, go to 19.

If the Sycorax stops, go to 43.

Everything goes dark and then, after a long moment, the lights come on and everything is quiet once more.

The soap bubble has now disappeared, leaving the equipment surrounding it shattered and destroyed.

The Doctor helps you and Amy to your feet.

Outside in the lab, you find the base crew recovering from their ordeal, now free of the Sycorax's control.

The Doctor quickly establishes what happened here.

Leaving the crew to get everything back to normal, the Doctor quietly leads you back towards the TARDIS.

'Seems that the shape-shifter crashed here in the Antarctic and this base was set up to recover the crashed spaceship. The Yarkop was injured in the crash, but managed to hide when the UNIT recovery team moved the crash remains to this base. When she recovered, she created a role for herself.'

'As a trainee nurse,' you say.

'Exactly,' continues the Doctor, 'she wanted to blend in while she worked out a way to get her stolen goods and herself off the planet.'

'But then the Sycorax arrived,' Amy guesses.

'Hot on her trail,' agrees the Doctor, 'and suddenly things got complicated.'

'Especially when the thing they were fighting over stole all the TARDIS energy and got you involved!' you point out.

You see that you've reached the TARDIS which is all lit up and fully recovered.

'Time to go home,' suggests the Doctor.

THE END

The Doctor tries to use the sonic screwdriver to loosen the screws and, after a moment's hesitation, all four screws respond and are soon in the Doctor's hand. He pulls the cover clear and places it at his feet. Beyond is a dark space. The Doctor reaches in and taps. CLANG! It's a metallic shaft, disappearing in a horizontal direction. The Doctor pokes his head into the hole and uses the sonic screwdriver to illuminate the shaft.

'Looks like it's horizontal for quite a way, but no guarantees – it could take a downward turn at any time.' He pulls his upper body back out of the hole and grins at you and Amy. 'Who's up for a magical mystery tour, then?' he asks.

Amy sighs. 'Go on then, I'll go first.'

The Doctor nods. 'And I'll bring up the rear,' he announces, as he helps Amy into the shaft. She quickly shuffles away into the darkness. The Doctor helps you follow her.

The shaft is dark and cold, but as you start to move along on your hands and knees, your eyes adjust to the lack of light and you are able to make out Amy, disappearing in the distance.

Keeping your head down to avoid banging it on the top of the shaft, you find yourself crashing into a wall in front of you. It's a T-junction. You look both ways but you can't see Amy.

If you go left, go to 52.

If you go right, go to 54.

The Doctor just laughs. 'You and Cathleen here are the only members of staff who didn't go into a coma,' he tells Yasin. 'Because you both never had blood samples taken. That's how they're controlling the others – they had access to their blood samples.'

'Who?' you ask the Doctor, 'who is controlling them?'

'I've got a very nasty idea,' he replies. 'Do you have any idea what this is you've got here?' He turns to Yasin.

Yasin looks a bit sheepish. 'To be honest – no. We know it's alien but that's about all,' he confesses.

The Doctor nods and runs a hand through his long fringe.

'What you've got here is an All Speed Inter-System Type K engine,' the Doctor tells him. 'Basically a crude bolt-on warp drive engine, which turns this chunk of old asteroid into a giant organic spaceship. As used by an unpleasant bunch of space scavengers called the Sycorax.'

'So is it the Sycorax who are controlling those poor people?' you wonder.

The Doctor leans against the nearest part of the engine, deep in thought.

Amy brings something across to him that she has found lying nearby. It looks a bit like a netbook computer with a simplified numerical keyboard and a screen.

'Brilliant,' says the Doctor. 'PCI – a personal computer interface. Let's see if we can get it to work.' He studies it for a moment. 'Now, if I remember correctly, the default access code is just PCI.'

If you want to use the computer yourself, click on box D on screen and enter the code word PCI.

If the Doctor enters the code, go to 27.

'A time machine? I don't believe you!' you splutter.

'Time and space machine, to be precise,' the Doctor adds. He wanders over to you and gives you back the screwdriver.

'Thanks,' he tells you.

You put it in your coat pocket and shake your head in disbelief. 'So you've got a time and space machine that fits into a small box but you don't have a screwdriver? How's that happen?'

The Doctor runs a hand through his hair and looks at you, appalled.

'Oh no, don't get the wrong idea. I've got a screwdriver, look.' He dashes back to the mushroom-shaped console and plucks a small metallic wand from a socket.

'It's sonic, actually, over four hundred settings according to the manual, but it's got one little drawback...'

'Short battery life?' you speculate.

'Can't handle Phillips head screws,' the Doctor confesses. 'Least not very well. And I always forget to pick one up when I'm on Earth.'

Amy laughs. 'Which is like, all the time. When do I get to see an alien planet then?'

'You've been to the past and to the future, what more do you want?' asks the Doctor.

'The past?' you ask.

'Yeah, World War Two. Hanging out with ol' Winnie.' Amy tells you with a grin.

'Winnie the Pooh?' you ask.

'Winston Churchill, of course,' she replies.

'Oh, right.' You try not to sound too disappointed.

The Doctor is looking at you with an amused smile on his face.

'Fancy a quick trip yourself?' he asks you. 'Back in time for tea, I promise you. Time machine, remember?'

If you say yes, go to 9.

If you hesitate, go to 40.

'What is it?' you ask the Doctor. The face you saw on the screen didn't seem to make sense — it appeared to be inside out, with a bone-like skull over exposed muscle, and no normal skin at all. You remember its angry red eyes and swallow hard.

'Sycorax,' the Doctor states. 'Nasty, superstitious, scavengers.'

'Not friendly aliens, then,' says Amy.

'Not in the slightest,' says the Doctor. 'I suspected their involvement when I saw those coma victims. They dress their science up like voodoo magic but blood control is one of their specialities. They stole the crew's blood samples then used them to put everyone in a coma.'

'But why?' you wonder.

The Doctor frowns. 'Don't know. But we'll find out soon enough. First we have to deal with this.'

He waves his hand at the equipment on the lone bench inside the glass room. It looks like some kind of science experiment with various bits and pieces of laboratory equipment circling a sparkling soap bubble.

'What is it? A breakthrough in soap bubble creation?' you joke, but the Doctor's face remains totally serious.

'It's a micro-universe being held in a stasis field,' he tells you solemnly. 'Believe me, that is more powerful than all the nuclear weapons on the planet put together.'

'Powerful *and* dangerous?' asks Amy.

If the Doctor answers Amy's question, go to 5.

If Nurse Cathleen screams, go to 61.

The lift doors open slowly to reveal a long curved corridor beyond. It is quite gloomy – there is some blue-tinged lighting from occasional recessed ceiling lamps, but the main lights are off.

'Emergency lights,' mutters the Doctor, as the three of you begin to explore.

'But what was the emergency?' wonders Amy.

The Doctor flashes her a quick grin. 'I dunno, it's a mystery isn't it? I love mysteries, don't you?'

As you explore the corridor you pass a number of doors. Each one appears to be locked, but most have glass panels in them which allow you to peer inside.

'This one's a gym,' you announce, looking through one such window and seeing exercise bikes, running machines and weights.

'And this looks like some kind of cafeteria,' adds Amy, looking through a door on the opposite side of the corridor.

'Exactly what you'd expect from some kind of research base in a remote spot like this,' comments the Doctor. 'There's just one thing missing...' he continues.

'People?' asks Amy.

The Doctor nods. 'The place is completely deserted, there's no sign of life at all. Quiet as the grave.'

Suddenly you hear the sound of movement beyond one of the doors.

The three of you exchange looks. The Doctor puts his finger to his lips and creeps towards the door. There is a small keypad next to the door. 'It needs a codeword,' he whispers. 'Try "Admin",' he suggests.

If you have access to a computer, click on box A on screen and enter the code word ADMIN.

If you do not, go to 30.

The Doctor enters the code and the screen comes to life.

The image that it shows is horrible. An alien face — humanoid, but with exposed red muscle under an outlying mass of bone, making it look inside out. Angry red eyes look out at you. The creature speaks, but the language is alien and ugly. Luckily the device has built-in translation, which appears in a pop-up box.

'Who are you and what do you want?' the machine types out.

'I want to help you,' says the Doctor, to your surprise.

It appears that the alien shares your surprise.

'We do not need help from inferior species,' it spits back.

'Well, one, I'm not anyone's "inferior species" and two, yes you do,' replies the Doctor steadily. 'Now let me make this easy for you. Your spaceship suffered a total power drain and crashed here, am I right?' The alien says nothing but nods very slightly. 'And without power you lost life support so you put your crew into suspended animation. But now your alarm has gone off and woken you up. Why is that?'

'Our last energy reserves were about to be drained,' the alien tells you via the translator.

'But luckily, while you were sleeping, this base arrived to investigate your ship. Giving you access to power and slave labour. So the question is — what do you need the humans on this base to do for you?'

If he answers the Doctor, go to 3.

If he hesitates, go to 82.

Amy runs to the door and opens it. She pops her head out and a moment later she stumbles back inside, slamming the door behind her. You can see a little snow on the floor of the TARDIS just inside the door.

'It's freezing out there. Seriously cold. Arctic,' she reports.

'Antarctic, to be precise,' the Doctor replies. 'According to these readings we're not far from the South Pole,' he continues. The screen he is looking at suddenly turns blank. 'That's the back-up power gone now. We need to get out of here.'

Amy looks horrified. 'Are you kidding? We'll freeze to death in minutes out there. Even without power we'd be better off in here.'

The Doctor shakes his head firmly. 'Don't you believe it.' From somewhere under the console he has produced a thick-set powerful torch which he flicks into life. The console room, now strangely dark and silent, feels as spooky as an abandoned cathedral. 'Follow me,' he instructs you and disappears through an internal door.

A few minutes later you are back in the console room but now you are all wearing snowsuits that the Doctor found for you in one of his massive wardrobe rooms. They are blue with white trim and look a bit like cool tracksuits. Although they seem to be comfortable and slightly padded they don't feel particularly thick.

'Trust me,' the Doctor assures you, 'you won't feel the cold.'

If you decide to exit the TARDIS first, go to 88.

If you let Amy go first, go to 62.

The Doctor takes a look at the nearest patient. Producing a stethoscope from somewhere, he listens to the man's heart and chest.

'Hmm, sounds normal,' he reports after a while, 'but he's definitely in a deep coma.'

Suddenly the door opens and a young woman in a neat white uniform enters. She looks a little flustered.

'Are you the relief medic?' she asks, in a strained voice.

'I am the Doctor,' the Doctor tells her, 'and you are...?'

'Trainee Nurse Cathleen Murphy,' she tells him, shaking his hand. The Doctor quickly introduces you and Amy.

'You're not the senior medic on the base, are you?' asks the Doctor gently.

'I shouldn't be,' confesses Cathleen, 'but that's Doctor Williams there,' she says, pointing to the far bed. 'And that's Doctor Kashta, Staff Nurse Pryor and Nurse Cato,' she continues, pointing to three more of the coma victims.

'All the senior medical staff came down with the same illness?' asks Amy, suspiciously.

'It's not really an illness, they just fell into comas without any reason,' Cathleen tells her.

'Can I see their medical notes?' asks the Doctor.

Cathleen looks a bit sheepish. 'They're all on the server. Only trouble is some of the data's been scrambled.'

She takes you across to a computer console. 'Just type in a name,' she tells you.

If you have access to a computer, click on box F on screen and enter the code word WILLIAMS.

If you do not, go to 73.

You type ADMIN into the keypad and instantly the door slides open. The Doctor steps through carefully and you and Amy follow him.

Something calls out in an alien tongue. The language is unrecognisable, but the tone is clear; the voice is angry and aggressive. The creature speaking is humanoid with red eyes and a face that looks inside out, with a skull-like exo-skeleton and exposed red muscle. It wears a sort of tribal uniform with swatches of bone, hair and skin hanging from its belt like trophies. In its hand it carries a whip-like weapon which crackles with an electrical charge.

The creature realises that you cannot understand his language and fiddles with a small piece of technology that hangs around his neck. When he speaks again his words are translated for you into a computerised voice that emerges from his necklace.

'We are Sycorax. We demand explanation for attack on our ship!' he states clearly.

The Doctor holds his hands up, in the universal gesture of peace.

'You and me both, we're in the same boat,' says the Doctor.

There is a pause while the translation software does its work in reverse. The electronic voice now repeats his words in the Sycorax tongue.

'Boat?' Seeing that the alien is confused, Amy tries to clarify the situation.

'We're travellers too. Our... er... spacecraft was drained of power. We're looking to find an explanation,' she tells them. 'Perhaps we can work together?'

If the alien agrees to Amy's suggestion, go to 85.

If the alien refuses to co-operate, go to 2.

You and Amy take the tunnel to the right and the Doctor disappears into the one on the left on his own.

Amy must be able to see the worry on your face because she gives your hand a reassuring squeeze and assures you that the Doctor will come back. 'He won't leave you,' she promises, 'Of course, sometimes it can take twelve years but he always comes back.' She sees your eyes widen at the reference to twelve years and gives your hand another squeeze. 'He only did that once. Don't worry. Now come on, let's get on with it, shall we?'

Holding her mobile phone up to give a little bit of light, she leads you on into the darkness. The passageway weaves through the rock and seems to get narrower the deeper you go.

'Funny kind of spaceship,' you comment, squeezing through a particularly narrow part of the tunnel.

'One thing I've learned already by travelling with the Doctor,' Amy begins, 'is that you should never be too surprised. The universe is full of such strange and magical things that it is always going to be weirder, more bizarre and more exciting than you can ever imagine. So you may as well get over being surprised because it's always surprising!'

'I think I can see some light,' you tell Amy, pushing past her and into the tunnel ahead.

If you continue along the tunnel, go to 99.

If you hear a familiar voice, go to 69.

The glass appears to be completely transparent, but when you walk around it, you find that you cannot see through to the other side.

'Hey, why can't I see through this glass?' you ask out loud.

The Doctor comes over for a closer look. 'Oh, that's very clever,' he decides after walking around the glass box a couple of times. 'How do you hide something in plain sight? Put it in an apparently empty box. Old magician's trick.'

Amy is standing with Cathleen. 'Did anyone ever tell you what is in there?' she asks.

Cathleen laughs. 'Me? No one ever tells me anything. All I know is that whatever is in there is the reason we're all here. It's that important.'

'Then it's important that we take a look inside,' says the Doctor. He takes out his sonic screwdriver and passes it through the air close to the glass, taking a reading of something. 'Hmm, traces of something there,' he mutters to himself. 'Artron energy.'

'What's that?' you ask him.

'It's time energy,' he tells you, 'and in the wrong hands it is a very dangerous thing indeed.' There is a door set into one of the four walls with a numerical keypad lock.

'I don't suppose you know the code for this?' asks the Doctor.

'Try 000,' suggests Cathleen, 'they can never remember PIN codes so they often reset things to that.'

If you have access to a computer, click on box E on screen and enter the code word 000.

If you do not, go to 56.

The Doctor runs across to the Professor, pulling his sonic screwdriver from his pocket.

'We haven't got much time,' he tells him, 'but I need access to your control systems. I need to jury rig a pulse wave modulator to activate the time-sensitive artron particles.'

The Professor just waves the Doctor towards the nearest computer. 'I've no idea what you're talking about but please, be my guest.'

The Doctor starts firing the sonic screwdriver at the computer and then sits and begins typing at incredible speed.

The Sycorax Warrior steps forwards to stand at his shoulder.

'Will this return power to my ship?' he demands.

The Doctor nods. 'But I want your word that you will leave this planet. It is protected and you are not welcome here.'

The Sycorax sneers. 'We do not want to be here anyway. Give me my ship and we will leave.'

'Can I trust a Sycorax?' asks the Doctor looking the alien in the eye.

'Can I trust humans?' responds the Sycorax, evenly.

'Guess you're going to have to,' says Amy, stepping between them. 'Get on with it then Doctor,' she suggests, and the Doctor returns to his work.

'Right,' he announces a moment later. 'When I press enter,

everything should get reversed...' he hesitates and then adds, 'I hope!'

'Enough talk,' insists the Sycorax and, pushing past the Doctor, he presses the button.

If the Doctor shouts out a warning, go to 74.

If blue lightning appears all over the Sycorax, go to 38.

Looking around the white, snowy plain you think you see something out of place.

'What's that, over there?' you call out, pointing in the direction of the odd object.

Amy frowns. 'I can't see anything,' she complains.

'Try these,' suggests the Doctor, handing you both a pair of tiny binoculars that he produces from one of his suit pockets.

You take the glasses and put them to your eyes. Instantly you get a much better view of what you saw and now it is much clearer that it isn't a part of the natural landscape.

'It's another crashed spaceship, isn't it?' you realise.

There are a couple of long elegant fins, like the spoilers on a classic car, but the main body of the ship appears to be a traditional flying saucer. It is stuck into the snow at a slight angle as if it landed rather badly.

'Unless I'm mistaken, that is a Mark Three Hopper,' the Doctor informs you, 'popular model for inter-system travel. You could say that it's the Ford Mondeo of spaceships.'

You and Amy just look at him.

'Just trying to put it in context for you,' the Doctor says, with a slightly pained expression.

'You sounded like Jeremy Clarkson,' Amy tells him, 'and that's not a good thing!'

'Looks like it crashed too, doesn't it?' you suggest.

The Doctor starts walking towards it. 'Only one way to find out!'

If you find the entrance, go to 51.

If the Doctor finds the entrance, go to 15.

The Doctor jumps in front of the Sycorax Warrior with his hands outstretched. 'No, wait! Stop, please,' he calls. To your surprise the Warrior does lower his arm.

'This creature is responsible for draining my ship of power,' the Sycorax states.

'Yes, but it's also the only hope you have of getting that energy back,' the Doctor tells him. 'Attack it and you'll never get off this planet.'

'Explain,' demands the electronic voice of the translation machine.

The Doctor takes a step towards the container and waves a hand at the pink blubbery creature.

'Our friend here is an Erali. They are deep space creatures who swim through the vacuum of space, often spending thousands of years between meals. So, like camels on this planet, they are built to store the food they might need between meals.'

'In the fat in their humps, right?' adds Amy. 'So this Erali just soaked up all our power because we happened to be passing?'

The Doctor nods. 'And it couldn't believe its luck. Two massive sources of energy. But it finds it hard to control its feeding systems. It couldn't stop itself draining the ships completely and now, now it's got the worst case of stomach ache ever.'

'Just like the Very Hungry Caterpillar?' you suggest.

The Doctor grins. 'Something along those lines; but the Erali won't be turning into a butterfly.'

'But how do we get the energy back?' wonders Amy.

'I'm a Time Lord, we've got remarkable control over our own biology.

I don't see why I can't help the Erali control hers. I just need to link up my mind with hers. So if you can just give me a minute...'

And without any further explanation, he calmly allows himself to fall backwards into the container, where he is instantly absorbed into the pink gloopiness.

A few moments later the surface of the liquid starts to bubble and shake as if coming to the boil. You and Amy take a step back. Suddenly there is a flash of blue/green light and you are temporarily blinded.

When you open your eyes again the Doctor is standing in the middle of the now empty circular container.

'Where is the Erali?' you ask.

'Gone,' the Doctor tells you with a smile, 'Back into space. Talking of which...' He turns to the Sycorax. 'Your ship is now refuelled and ready to leave. Don't miss your flight.' The Warrior fixes his whip to his belt and turns on his heel without a further word.

'So why was the Erali here?' you wonder.

'She got lost and fell to Earth,' the Doctor tells you, 'and the scientists at this base found her and tried to examine her. Unfortunately when they tried to X-Ray her she panicked and gave off an energy shock wave that accidently killed everyone on the base.' The Doctor looks grim. 'This base should be abandoned and forgotten, don't you think? Time to go...'

If you lead the way, go to 12.

If Amy leads the way, go to 55.

36

A man in a white lab coat appears from behind one of the pieces of machinery. He is thin and pale and his sparse hair sticks up at a strange angle.

The Sycorax Warrior lifts up his whip weapon but the Doctor grabs his arm.

'Hold on – how about we ask questions first, eh?' Nimbly the Doctor steps in front of the alien and approaches the man in the white coat.

The man looks frightened but a little more at ease with the human-looking Doctor.

'What's going on here?' asks the Doctor.

'I don't know...' stammers the man.

The Sycorax raises his whip again but the Doctor waves him down. 'Let me guess... this is an energy research base, am I right?' says the Doctor.

The man nods. 'My name is Professor Gerald Howkins, and this is my project. Project Energise.' The man throws his hands wide to indicate the whole base, but there's little pride in the gesture. He looks a broken man.

'But it's all gone terribly wrong,' he confesses, collapsing into a plastic chair near one of the many computer work stations dotted amongst the machines. The Doctor is looking around at the bits of equipment.

'So what we have here is some kind of energy magnet, right?' he asks.

The Professor looks up, the surprise he feels written all over his face.

'Yes, but how could you possibly know that?'

If the Sycorax leader wields his whip, go to 87.

If the Doctor wants to hear more, go to 11.

37

You decide to take the left hand corridor. The Doctor leads the way.

'Where are the crew?' you wonder.

'Good question,' the Doctor answers you, 'but I don't have an answer. 'Although, despite its size, this ship might not have a very large crew. Most of the systems are automated.'

'But there must be some people on board,' says Amy. 'More aliens like old Skull-face?'

The Doctor shrugs. 'I don't know. But I know I have a bad feeling about this. Don't you?'

You shudder involuntarily. Has it got a bit colder? A thought strikes you.

'Is it possible that something on this ship caused the power drain?' you ask.

'Anything is possible,' the Doctor tells you.

It's hard to be sure because the ship isn't lying quite horizontally but you appear to have been descending gently as you walk along the curved corridor. Suddenly you come to a bulkhead door that is closed. The view panel in the middle of the door is blackened glass, impossible to see through.

Next to the door is a small numeric keypad.

The Doctor gets his sonic screwdriver out but quickly shakes his head. 'Sonic can't break it, we need the code.'

'Maybe it's not been set, maybe it just has the factory default, like a phone does,' you suggest.

'What, like 7890?' says Amy.

'Why not?' grins the Doctor.

If you have access to a computer, click on box B on screen and enter the code 7890.

If you do not, go to 20.

The Sycorax Warrior is staggering around inside a web of sparkling blue electricity that is running all over his body. The Doctor fires a blast from the sonic screwdriver and pulls a strand of the blue energy away from the alien and on to a nearby metal filing cabinet. He then runs over to the cabinet and, after changing the setting, he lets his sonic screwdriver stick to the side of it.

'It's magnetic?' you ask him.

'It's a lot of things,' the Doctor tells you. 'Right now, it's bait.'

As you watch, the blue energy that is streaming over the Sycorax's frame starts to move away, as if drawn along the strand of lightning that leads to the cabinet. In seconds it is the cabinet that has the energy swirling all over it and the alien is free. He looks at the Doctor, confused but grateful.

'Don't mention it,' the Doctor tells him quickly before turning back to the larger problem. 'Right, we need to reverse the energy drain, repower our ships and stop this place disappearing in a hole in time and space big enough to swallow the entire solar system,' he announces. 'Any ideas?' The Doctor looks around the room frantically. 'What I need is access to the core of the scope. If I can reverse the polarity of the neutron flow...'

The Doctor runs across to a panel in the central machine in the room. 'Just one problem,' he announces, pointing at the screws securing the access panel, 'sonic screwdriver's tied up keeping that energy leak at bay and I need to unscrew this panel.'

You fish something out of your pocket. 'Would this help?' you ask, handing over the screwdriver you lent the Doctor back on Earth.

'Perfect.' The Doctor quickly opens up the panel and disappears into the heart of the machine. Moments later he gives a cry of triumph and emerges.

'Well?' Amy demands.

'Bad news; your screwdriver got lashed into my fix and it's going to have to stay there,' he tells you, 'but the good news is – it worked!'

He goes over to the Sycorax and helps him up. 'Your ship has power. Now, leave this planet.'

The Sycorax walks to the door then turns and nods his head in acknowledgement before spinning around and leaving.

'We'd better be going too,' the Doctor says, walking over to the Professor. 'But I think you need to look elsewhere for new energy sources. You can't just get free energy by stealing it.'

'No, I can see that,' the Professor tells him, clearly shaken by his experiences.

The Doctor leans closer and whispers. 'Don't tell anyone I said this, but you might like to look into neutronic flow systems to build better energy storage. Good luck.'

The Doctor turns back to you and Amy. 'Right – TARDIS and home.'

Amy sees the expression on your face. 'Maybe we can build a snowman first?' she suggests.

The Doctor looks at you both and then grins. 'Okay.'

THE END

All of the coma patients are now out of their beds and staggering towards you, like zombies or sleepwalkers. Their eyes are open but they don't seem to be able to see. They are converging on the four of you with their arms outstretched.

'Doctor,' Amy says tersely, 'let's get out of here.' You feel the door behind you and quickly open it. The four of you tumble through the open doorway and run off down the corridor, not looking back to see if you are being chased.

Cathleen runs with you. The trainee nurse looks absolutely terrified. 'What's happening?' she manages to ask.

'I was rather hoping that you might tell us,' the Doctor tells her.

'I mean with the patients?' she insists.

'Oh that,' says the Doctor casually, 'that's easy. Bio-feedback control through blood. Crude but clever. I've seen something like it before a few Christmases back.'

Amy checks behind you.

'I don't think they're following,' she tells you.

You stop running and gather your breath.

'So what exactly is this base for?' asks the Doctor.

Cathleen smiles wryly. 'I can't really tell you without authorisation from the base commander.'

'So let's go find her,' says Amy. Her face falls. 'Don't tell me it's a bloke. Why is it always a bloke in charge?'

'Actually our commander is a woman,' Cathleen tells her. 'You've already met her. She was in bed four!'

'Is the whole crew in a coma?' you ask.

Cathleen nods. 'All but me.'

'And you never had a blood sample taken with the rest?'

the Doctor guesses.

'I took everyone else's when we arrived but I forgot to do myself,' she confesses.

'Leaving you the last man standing and the only hope of helping us get to the bottom of this. So, what's the base all about?'

'Why don't I show you?' she suggests and leads you to a lift which takes you down to a lower level of the base.

Inside the lift Cathleen begins to explain a little more about where you are.

'We're ten metres below the surface in the Antarctic,' she tells you. 'The base was originally designed to enable a team of experts to study and measure the effects of global warming, but a few months ago it was reassigned and taken over by a team of international experts pulled together by some secret organisation called UNIT.'

You and Amy have never heard of it, but the Doctor instantly breaks into a grin.

'So what do my old friends at UNIT want an Antarctic base for?' he wonders.

The lift comes to a stop and the doors open. Beyond is a bright, modern laboratory full of high-tech state-of-the-art equipment. There is a small glass-sided room in the middle of floor.

You move out of the lift and begin to look around. The Doctor immediately moves across to look to take a closer look at the glass room.

If the glass is clear, go to 32.

If the glass is opaque, go to 80.

'A trip, in this thing?'

'It really can go anywhere in time and space,' insists the Doctor.

'Just mostly Earth in my experience,' Amy mutters, in a whisper that's just a bit too loud.

Suddenly the Doctor is at the control console. He dances around the various panels prodding at buttons and flicking switches apparently at random.

'Come on then, let's get moving.'

He pulls a lever and from somewhere deep below you ancient engines begin to growl. A noise akin to a screaming elephant fills the room.

'Hold on,' warns Amy, 'his take-offs can be a little shaky.'

'Hey, don't diss the driver,' retorts the Doctor, grinning, but never taking his eyes off the various dials and readouts.

Suddenly the noise reaches a crescendo and then everything becomes calm, save for a background rhythmic hum that makes the ship sound somehow alive.

'So, how long does it take?' you wonder.

'How long is a piece of string?' replies the Doctor with a laugh.

'In other words, he doesn't know,' Amy tells you.

Without warning the floor beneath your feet shudders and you fall into Amy.

'What's that?' you ask, as a sonorous bell begins to toll loudly.

'Bad news,' mutters the Doctor.

You can see from Amy's face that she has never heard this sound before.

'Is something going wrong?' you ask her.

If Amy answers, go to 59.

If the Doctor answers, go to 66.

The Sycorax is about to continue his explanation when suddenly there is a terrible screaming noise and the image breaks up. The screen goes blank and then there is a long moment of silence.

'What happened?' you wonder.

'I think the energy eater just caught up with him,' mutters the Doctor, looking grim.

'But you can stop it, right?' asks Amy.

'Of course,' the Doctor answers her confidently, before rather spoiling the effect by adding, 'I think so. Put it this way, I'm working on a plan.'

'Working on!'

'Trust me, by the time we find the thing I'll have a plan all worked out,' he assures her.

He goes over to examine the Sycorax engine. 'This all looks in order. If we can just reverse the energy drain, this engine can launch the ship back into space without too much trouble.'

'What about the base above?' asks Cathleen.

'Get up there and evacuate the place,' suggests the Doctor. 'You have emergency shelters?' Cathleen nods. The Doctor continues his orders, 'the coma patients should have been released by now. They'll be groggy but capable of doing what they need to do.'

'Don't we need all the help we can get to capture this thing?' you ask.

'Who said anything about capturing it?' says the Doctor with a cheeky grin. 'I was thinking more along the lines of having a chat.'

If the Doctor needs to use the netbook some more, go to 64.

If he sets off into the caves, go to 93.

The lift comes to a halt, but the doors fail to open.

You and Amy exchange nervous glances.

The Doctor just steps forward and gives the doors a bang with his fist. Slowly the doors begin to open and the Doctor grabs both of them and gives them a hand to open fully.

Beyond the lift is a long, curved corridor, lit only by occasional blue ceiling lights. The main lights are off.

'Emergency lighting?' wonders Amy, as you begin to explore.

'Or it might be night-time,' says the Doctor. 'An enclosed base like this needs to maintain a day/night cycle for the sake of its occupants.'

You begin to walk along the corridor, passing a number of doors as you move. Each door has an observation panel built in, enabling you to peer through to the darkened rooms beyond.

You find a gym, full of exercise bikes and other typical equipment, and a communal eating area with vending machines.

'Wonder where the people are?' says the Doctor.

Without warning you hear something crash in one of the nearby rooms. Instantly you all freeze. The Doctor gestures you to keep quiet and tiptoes towards the room where it happened.

There is a small keyboard next to the door, with the letters of the alphabet on it.

'What would the password be?' mutters the Doctor. 'Penguin, Antarctic... Or maybe they never got round to setting one. Try ADMIN.'

If you have access to a computer, click on box A on screen and enter the code word ADMIN.

If you do not, go to 30.

43

The Sycorax Warrior hesitates and looks at the Doctor.

'Don't touch the crystal,' the Doctor repeats. 'It's dangerous.'

The Sycorax bares its teeth and hisses at him. 'You think I am afraid?'

'No, not afraid, just stupid... Listen to me...' the Doctor insists.

The Sycorax pushes him away violently and turns back to the crystal. 'This will be mine!' he announces and reaches out to touch his glittery prize.

As soon as he is in contact with the crystal, you can see from his expression that he knows he has made a mistake. Before he can say anything, however, a paralysis completely overcomes him.

Amy helps the Doctor get to his feet. He pulls a face, upset that the alien failed to listen to him.

'What did that crystal do to him?' Amy asks.

'Unhooked him from time,' the Doctor tells you, 'just like this green lot.' He indicates the aliens. 'They've all been cut off from normal time and left in a sort of super-slow time. They're alive, but living life a million times slower than usual.'

'So who are these guys?' you ask, taking a closer look at the green-skinned aliens.

'Atraians, they're traders,' the Doctor answers you. 'They travel all over the place buying and selling products from other cultures. Not so different to the Sycorax really, just a bit more honest about it. They must have picked this H'R'R'lurrniki Energy Converter up without really understanding what it was they had taken aboard.'

'And what exactly is it?' asks Amy, walking slowly around the crystal, while keeping a safe distance from it.

'Semi-organic energy storage, created by the Master Cultivators of the H'R'R'lurrniki Cluster. Wonderful garden centres on

H'R'R'lurrniki Prime.'

'So what went wrong? Why is it time-freezing people?' you wonder.

'My fault, I fear. The TARDIS passed in range and the crystal couldn't resist the artron energy inside. Trouble is, artron energy is time-active and very difficult to contain. Now it's venting artron energy and causing these pockets of slow time.'

'So turn it off,' suggests Amy,

'Easier said than done,' the Doctor tells her. 'But I'll give it a go. Now, in theory, as a time-sensitive I should be able to resist the artron leakage and commune telepathically with the crystal's control systems. If I'm wrong...'

He stops and flashes you a quick grin. 'Stick me in a nice garden somewhere!' With that he reaches out and touches the crystal.

For a long moment nothing happens and then reality seems to warp in front of your eyes. Suddenly everything begins to spin as if being sucked into a giant whirlpool and then, thankfully, you pass out.

When you come round, you are lying on the floor in the TARDIS. Amy is close by. The Doctor, seeing that you are awake, helps you to your feet.

'What happened?' you wonder.

'It worked,' the Doctor tells you, grinning. 'I reversed the energy flow and let the artron energy reset time. The Sycorax and the Atraians have gone back into space and that research base is safe.'

'So what happens now?' you ask.

'Time to go home,' says the Doctor. 'Let's see how many attempts it takes to get you there!'

THE END

44

To your surprise the patient nearest to the door just reaches up to the keypad and punches in the access code. The door begins to open.

The Doctor fires his sonic screwdriver again and the door closes.

With almost comic inevitability, the zombie patient reaches for the keypad again. Once again the door begins to open. Unfortunately the slow-moving coma patients can't walk fast enough to enter the glass room before the Doctor closes the door again.

All of the zombies turn to look at the Doctor.

'I can do this all day, you know,' he says with a grin, holding up the sonic screwdriver.

Suddenly the sonic screwdriver is whipped out of his hand by a sparkling, blue electronic whip.

You turn and see a red-robed alien with a bony head wielding the whip.

'The Sycorax!' says the Doctor, not at all surprised. 'Knew you'd be around here somewhere. Blood control and all that, dead giveaway.'

The alien says something but his language is impossible to understand.

Suddenly the nearest zombie patient begins to speak for him.

'Do not interfere,' it says.

'Oh that's new,' says the Doctor, 'using your puppets as organic translators. Good, we can talk now.'

'I have nothing to speak with your inferior species about,' says the Sycorax through the mouth of the zombie. 'Do not stand between me and my prize,' he adds.

If he explains what his prize is, go to 10.

If the Doctor guesses what his prize is, go to 86.

45

You hand over the screwdriver, which you have borrowed from home. When the Doctor stopped you in the street and asked for help you'd been surprised by his request and even more surprised when he'd headed off into the blue box. Those surprises had just been the beginning though. When you had stepped through the doors of the "police box" (whatever a police box was) you found yourself in this incredibly vast room.

'Ah, fantastic,' says the Doctor, taking the screwdriver and then stopping suddenly with a frown. 'No, that's not right. Not one of my words any more. Sorry. Oh, and there's another. Said enough of those too...'

You look over at the pretty Scottish girl. She smiles back, kindly.

'Don't worry,' she tells you, 'he's always like this. I'm Amy by the way and that's...'

'The Doctor,' finishes the Doctor, glancing up from whatever it is he is doing with your screwdriver. 'I've already done that bit,' he adds, looking at Amy.

'And have you explained about this place – the TARDIS?' she asks him.

The Doctor looks pained. 'I was just asking to borrow a screwdriver, not telling my life story. Or should that be life stories?'

Amy shakes her head and comes over to you. 'This is the TARDIS,' she tells you, waving a hand around as if she were showing off her flat, 'it's a time machine.'

If you ask to go back in time, go to 97.

If you don't believe her, go to 24.

46

You step out through the TARDIS doors. Part of you thinks this is all some kind of joke and that you will find yourself back in the street where you came from, but you soon see that the TARDIS really has transported you somewhere else.

'Wow! One small step for man...' you mutter and then you look around you and your voice drops away. This isn't the moon, or a medieval village, or a starliner in deep space; instead you appear to have arrived in a grey, nondescript corridor. It looks like an office building, or behind the scenes at a shopping mall. There are metallic skirting boards, a thin grey lino on the floor, and exposed breeze blocks make up the walls.

You realise that Amy and the Doctor have followed you out and have started to explore.

'Ah, this looks interesting,' announces the Doctor. You see that he is looking through the glass window of a door that is labelled with a familiar red cross.

'Some kind of medical centre?' you suggest.

The Doctor nods. 'Good job I'm a Doctor then,' he says and then enters the room.

You and Amy follow and find yourselves in a small medical ward. There are about twelve beds in the room and each of them is occupied.

All of the patients seem to be in a deep coma.

'Can't be contagious or they'd be in isolation,' comments the Doctor, 'So I wonder what's wrong with them?'

If the Doctor starts to examine one of the patients, go to 29.

If the door opens and someone enters, go to 57.

Amy claps her hands. 'Easy – you two are the only ones who didn't go into a coma. The aliens could only control those whose blood it had, is that right? Like voodoo or something.'

'It's not voodoo or magic, just science, but yes,' agrees the Doctor, 'that is how they are controlling the poor patients that chased us.'

'But who is pulling the strings?' you ask.

'That's easy. This is an All Speed Inter-System Type K starship engine.'

'You mean this rock is a spaceship?' asks Amy, trying to make sense of what the Doctor has said.

'The usual transport of a bunch of galactic traders and scavengers called the Sycorax. Superstitious, violent and weirdly mystic to boot. And yet they end up being one of the longest surviving species in the universe,' the Doctor tells you, 'right up there with cockroaches.'

The Doctor notices something lying near the engine and bends to pick it up. It appears to be some kind of netbook. It opens to display a screen showing a simplified numerical keyboard.

'What's that?' you ask.

'Known as a PCI, it's the next big thing in personal computers and it launches in 2012, so spoilers you two, don't let on when you get home!' says the Doctor. 'Right, this is a mark 3 so the default access code is simply PCI.'

If you want to use the computer yourself, click on box D on screen and enter the code word PCI.

If the Doctor enters the code, go to 27.

The Doctor opens the door with a quick blast of his sonic screwdriver. 'Deadlock sealed,' he mutters and then breaks into a grin. 'Joking!' He steps inside.

Amy rolls her eyes in exasperation and waves at you to go ahead of her. When she follows you through the door she pulls it shut behind her.

Inside the igloo is a lobby with lift doors which reminds you of a multi-storey car park. The curved inside wall of the igloo can now be seen to be constructed from a number of larger curved panels, bolted together to form the structure. The lift doors and shaft are the only features of the room. There are no signs or labels of any kind.

The Doctor sonics the control panel next to the lift and, from some distance below you, a buzzing sound starts up. A few moments later the lift doors slide open to reveal a spacious, but plain, lift cage.

'Going down?' suggests the Doctor, bouncing eagerly into the lift.

'Is there any other option?' retorts Amy, as you join the Doctor in the lift.

As soon as the three of you are inside, the lift the doors shut and you begin to descend. The Doctor starts counting silently, his lips moving without making any noise.

'50 metres,' he announces when the lift comes to a halt after a few seconds, 'give or take a centimetre or two. Deep. Very deep.'

If the doors open automatically, go to 26.

If the doors stay closed, go to 42.

The Doctor watches the two Sycorax circling each other, considering his next move, then suddenly he runs out between them, holding his hands out and screaming 'Stop!' To everyone's surprise, they do. Then both growl threateningly and bare their teeth at the Doctor.

'Yes, yes,' says the Doctor trying not to sound too frightened, 'it's a very good impression, but if we don't just calm down someone is going to get seriously hurt.'

'Are you volunteering, little man?' asks one of the Sycorax Leaders — the one who is armed with an energy whip.

The Doctor suddenly grins and, reaching forwards, snatches the whip out of the totally surprised alien's hands. 'Hey, that's mine,' he complains, as the Doctor dances quickly away, tossing the whip from one hand to the other.

'Nice speech,' he says to the disarmed Sycorax, 'shame the genuine article won't use any Terran languages. Bit of a giveaway.' The Doctor turns and tosses the whip away before turning back to the fake alien.

'Now listen to me,' he says, suddenly very serious, 'you need to return the energy you stole. All of it. Both the power from this Sycorax ship and the stuff you took from mine. Mine is a very special space-time craft and the artron energy you stole will kill you if you don't.'

Unseen by anyone, the real Sycorax bends to pick up his whip.

If the creature changes back to its natural form, go to 72.

If he remains a Sycorax, go to 16.

Amy pats you on the back. 'You were right. The answer is right under our noses,' she tells you.

'In fact, it's right under our feet,' adds the Doctor.

You see that he has dropped to his knees and is scrabbling at the snow with both hands, like a dog burying a bone. Suddenly he stops and reaches into the hole that he has made.

CLANG! A metallic knock.

You step closer and peer over the Doctor's shoulder. At the bottom of the hole in the snow is a metal plate.

'What is it?' you ask.

'Not sure yet,' says the Doctor jumping to his feet and starting to move away. He pulls his sonic screwdriver from an inner pocket and begins to wave it over the ground. A blue light flashes at the end of the rod. 'According to the sonic screwdriver it's pretty big, though.'

'There's not much that thing can't do,' Amy tells you, grinning, 'except unscrew a cross-headed screw of course!'

The Doctor glares at her and Amy laughs.

'Don't look so upset, I wasn't dissing the sonic screwdriver.'

'Good, 'cos it's just come up trumps again,' he tells her, grinning just as broadly, 'Look, I've found an entrance.'

The Doctor has discovered what appears to be a snow igloo on the snowy plain, but closer examination shows it to be some kind of plastic, with a metallic door.

If the door is locked, go to 48.

If the door is unlocked, go to 79.

As you get closer to the crashed ship, you realise how big it is. It's about the size of a small warehouse. You see something that could be an airlock and call the others over.

It is an entrance of some kind, but there is no clue as to how to make it open.

The Doctor pulls out his sonic screwdriver and gives it a blast. Slowly the door opens, sliding up to reveal an airlock beyond. Once the three of you are inside the outer door closes again and you suddenly begin to feel warm.

'It's hot in here!' you exclaim, feeling rather uncomfortable.

'Don't worry,' the Doctor tells you, 'these suits are temperature regulators, they can cool you as easily as keep you warm.' He makes an adjustment to the controls on the front of your suit and you instantly feel much more comfortable.

'Have you noticed anything?' the Doctor asks, as he makes a similar adjustment to Amy's suit.

'Like it's warm in here?' you answer.

'Sort of.' The Doctor turns and operates a control to open the inner door of the airlock. Beyond is a small lobby with two corridors leading off it, one to the left and one to the right. 'It's warm in here, because life support is working. As is the airlock. As are the lights...'

You realise what he's saying. 'The power's on!'

'So this ship isn't another victim of the power drain,' adds Amy.

If you go left, go to 37.

If you go right, go to 77.

Suddenly you turn to the left and find the shaft dropping away beneath you, as it becomes vertical rather than horizontal. Luckily the shaft levels out again, before bending and curving like a swimming pool water slide. You hurtle along it, powered by the energy of your first drop, bouncing off the smooth metal sides of the shaft.

Finally the shaft ends and you hurtle out of it and find yourself landing on something soft.

'Ow!' Amy is not impressed. It is Amy that you have landed on.

'Quick! Out of the way,' you tell her and the pair of you roll to one side just in time, as a second later the Doctor shoots out of the end of the pipe but, unlike either you or Amy, he somehow manages to land on his feet. He adjusts his tie and brushes the hair off his forehead.

'That was fun,' he mutters. 'Now where are we?'

'You have arrived just in time to see me end this farce,' says a familiar electronic voice.

You and Amy get to your feet. You are in a fairly dark, large and mainly empty room. The Sycorax Warrior is here and he is standing over what looks like a large inflatable swimming pool filled with pink blancmange.

Then you realise that the pink substance is moving and changing shape – it seems to be alive.

The Doctor hurries over. The Sycorax raises his whip, ready to attack the pink creature.

If the Doctor stops him in time, go to 35.

If the Doctor doesn't reach him in time, go to 67.

Soon there is a pitched snowball fight going on; all three of you laughing and smiling and hurling snow at each other.

You manage to get both the Doctor and Amy with a giant snowball and suddenly find yourself being chased by them both. The snow boots that go with the suits are bulky and uncomfortable but they grip the snowy surface well and you are soon putting some distance between yourself and your pursuers. You glance back to see where they are and are surprised to see that they have stopped.

You turn back to look where you are going and skid to an urgent stop. There is something very out of place in front of you. It looks for a moment like a mountain in the middle of the snow but there are no flakes of snow on any of the rugged rocky surfaces of the object. In fact, if anything, it appears to be rather hot. Around its base pools of water have formed and when you reach a hand towards the craggy surface you can feel the heat coming off it.

The Doctor and Amy have joined you now, the snowball fight forgotten.

'What is it?' you ask them.

Amy shakes her head. 'Exactly what it looks like – a great big rock.'

The Doctor doesn't agree. 'It doesn't belong here at all. It's alien.'

'Someone brought it here from somewhere else?' you wonder.
'I mean someone crashed it here,' the Doctor tells you.

If you hear a new voice, go to 17.

If the Doctor explains the rock, go to 68.

You turn to the right and carry on crawling. Without warning the shaft suddenly drops away and you start to fall. A moment later and you are falling out of the end of the shaft and dropping into a new room. Luckily your fall is broken by a pile of plastic bags filled with something soft.

'It's rice,' Amy tells you. 'I think we're in a storeroom.'

You quickly scramble off the bags of rice just in time, before the Doctor comes hurtling out of the pipe. He has his hands crossed over his chest and his feet straight out in front of him, just like someone riding a water slide at an amusement park. He bounces twice on his bottom and then dismounts from the rice bags like a gymnast.

'How's that?' he asks, as he completes his landing.

'Ten marks for execution, nine marks for style,' Amy tells him.

'Where are we?' you ask, more practically.

The Doctor takes a quick look around. 'Basement level – food storage... I wonder what else they keep down here.'

He leads the way to a door and sonics it open.

The next room is even bigger and quite dark. There is a large object in the middle of the room – a circular container about ten metres wide and about a metre tall. It reminds you of a penguin enclosure at a zoo.

If you decide to take a closer look, go to 70.

If Amy takes a closer look, go to 7.

Amy leads the way and it seems like no time at all before you are back in the lift cage, rising this time, heading back to the igloo lobby where you left the high-tech cold weather clothing that the Doctor found for you in the TARDIS. Soon you have pulled on the thin but effective overalls and the massive snow boots and you are ready to step out once again into the snowy wastelands of the Antarctic.

When you get outside, you see that it has been snowing again and the indentation that shows where the Sycorax Asteroid ship had crashed is already beginning to fill in with fresh snow.

'There they go,' says the Doctor, looking up into the sky, but you can't see which of the many stars might be the Sycorax ship.

'So many stars,' you comment.

'And those are just the ones you can see,' the Doctor tells you.

'Look, the ship!' cries Amy.

You spin around to see where she is pointing. The TARDIS is lit up and seems brighter than ever.

'Looks like the power's back on,' comments the Doctor, striding towards his ship.

You look sideways at Amy. 'Just one thing before we go... it seems a shame to waste all this snow. Can't we have a little play?'

Amy grins.

Half an hour later it is finally time to go. When the TARDIS fades from view on the Antarctic plain, you leave behind one fantastic snowman, dressed in some bits and bobs from the Doctor's amazing wardrobe room; a floppy felt hat and an enormous multi-coloured scarf.

THE END

The Doctor enters the numerals "000" on the numerical keypad and there is a satisfying CLUNK as the lock is released. Slowly, the door slides open.

The Doctor leads the way into the room and you and Amy hurry after him. To your surprise, it is dark in the room, save for a long, low-hanging blue-tinted lamp that hands over the only significant piece of furniture, a long laboratory table.

On the table there is something that initially looks like a child's toy. It consists of a frame built from miniature scaffolding on which wires, lenses and other equipment have been clamped, all focused around a central raised circular platform. Hovering above the platform, suspended by invisible forces, is what looks like a soap bubble. Inside the soap bubble, which is about three centimetres across, you can see pinpricks of bright light and a swirling grey/blue mist.

The Doctor takes a closer look.

You and Amy exchange puzzled glances.

'This is incredible,' the Doctor breathes, staring so closely at the soap bubble that he begins to go cross-eyed.

'It's very pretty, but what is it?'

'Totally impossible, for one thing,' the Doctor tells you. 'It's a micro-universe. A little part of another universe held in a stasis field.

No wonder there was an energy drain. The power needed to maintain this is enormous.'

'Is it dangerous?' asks Amy.

If the Doctor answers Amy's question, go to 5.

If Nurse Cathleen screams, go to 61.

Before the Doctor can take a closer look at one of the patients, a door at the far end of the ward opens and a young woman comes hurrying into the room.

'Oh, thank goodness,' she says, seeing the three of you standing there. 'Which one of you is the Doctor?'

Hiding his surprise, the Doctor tells the woman that he is the Doctor and goes on to introduce you and Amy.

The woman, who introduces herself as Trainee Nurse Cathleen Murphy, is looking very relieved. 'Control said the relief medic and his team might not be with us for days. I guess the snowstorms must have died down.'

'Are you in charge here?' asks Amy.

'By default,' confesses Cathleen. 'Doctor Williams and Doctor Kashta are over there,' she says, indicating two of the patients, 'and Staff Nurse Pryor and Nurse Cato are in these two beds here,' she adds, waving a hand at two of the beds on the other side of the room.

'So all of the senior medical team contracted the same illness. Shouldn't they be in isolation?' you ask.

'Perhaps you should read the files,' Cathleen suggests. 'They're online but you might encounter some data problems.' She takes you to a console. 'Just type in one of the patients' names,' she says.

If you have access to a computer, click on box F on screen and enter the code word WILLIAMS.

If you do not, go to 73.

Without hesitating, the Doctor steps out and positions himself between the two antagonists. 'Stop!' he cries, holding his hands out flat. The two Sycorax bear their teeth in unison and emit a low growling noise. 'Oh, very good,' comments the Doctor. 'Great impression, very lifelike – but if you don't back off, someone's going to get hurt.'

One of the Sycorax Leaders – the one who is holding an energy whip in his hands – laughs. 'And it will be you, little man!' he says, brandishing the whip.

'I'll have that, thank you,' the Doctor says, producing his sonic screwdriver and using it to yank the whip out of the alien's hands. Deftly the Doctor catches the leather grip of the whip weapon and, to your surprise, he hands it to the other Sycorax. 'Yours I believe, taken by our friend here along with your identity.'

The Sycorax who has just been given the whip nods an acknowledgement as the Doctor turns back to face the now disarmed imposter.

'This needs to end now,' he tells the shape-shifter. 'You took too much energy, way too much. Give it back before it burns you up. What you stole from my space-time ship isn't your run-of-the-mill

energy, mine's time energy. If you don't send it back, it will kill you.
Trust me, I know.'

**If the creature changes back to its natural form,
go to 72.**

If he remains a Sycorax, go to 16.

59

Amy looks at you and shrugs. 'I'm not really an expert,' she tells you. 'I've only had a few trips in this thing myself!'

The Doctor is moving purposefully around the console, checking readings and flicking the odd switch with a grim determination.

'This is completely mad,' he mutters. 'We're losing all power.'

'What do you mean?' you ask.

The Doctor just looks at you wide-eyed, his hair falling over his brow again. 'It's like something is sucking every last bit of energy out of the TARDIS.'

'Like squeezing juice out of a lemon?' suggests Amy.

'But nothing should be able to interfere with TARDIS systems like that. Not even the combined hordes —'

'Of Genghis Khan could get through those doors,' Amy completes the sentence for him. 'You mentioned it before.'

'I'm going to need a new line,' says the Doctor, turning back to the controls. 'Right, hold on you two, this might be a tad rocky. Emergency Materialisation...'

The Doctor pulls down a lever and instantly the pitch of the TARDIS engines changes. The groaning trumpeting you heard before fills the air, but this time it sounds strained, desperate.

The floor is vibrating, shaking, and you and Amy have to hold on to an upright firmly to remain on your feet.

Suddenly there is a deep booming sound and all is still. A moment later the lights begin to fade.

'Oh dear,' mutters the Doctor.

If Amy runs to the door, go to 28.

If the Doctor runs to the door, go to 60.

60

The Doctor runs to the door and opens it.

'Just wait here,' he tells you and disappears.

You and Amy are left looking at each other in the rapidly darkening control room. The lights have all but faded now and the console itself looks rather dead and lifeless.

'Maybe he just needs a new tank of fuel,' you wonder.

Amy smiles but you can see that she is worried.

'I don't think it takes Unleaded,' she tells you.

To your relief the door opens again and the Doctor reappears.

'What's out there?' you demand.

'Where have we landed then?' asks Amy.

'Is it safe?' you wonder.

The Doctor stops, blinks and then answers. 'In reverse order, don't know, don't know and some kind of base.'

You hesitate for a moment, running the questions back in your mind and assigning the Doctor's answers to the right questions. Amy is quicker at this than you.

'What kind of base?' she asks. 'Moon base, deep sea base, Homebase?'

The Doctor shrugs. 'Some kind of self-contained facility, built for humanoids probably humans. Recycled air, dead give away, you can taste it. So could be anywhere but likely to be in a hostile environment of some kind. Gravity feels Earth normal, but that's common.'

'So it could be another planet?' you wonder.

'But it's most likely Earth, right?' says Amy.

The Doctor grins. 'Only one way to find out.'

If the Doctor leads the way out, go to 13.

If you lead the way out, go to 46.

The scream is high-pitched and full of fear. Without hesitating you all run back through the still-open sliding door to see what is scaring Cathleen so badly.

As soon as you come round the edge of the glass cube, you skid to a halt. The coma patients have arrived and a group of them have backed a terrified Cathleen into a corner.

'Help me — do something!' she shouts out, petrified with fear.

'Don't panic,' suggests the Doctor.

'Easy for you to say!' Cathleen screams back at him.

'Just stand still,' he says. 'They won't harm you.'

Biting her lip and closing her eyes, Cathleen stands still. You see that she has crossed her fingers.

The zombies stop moving, too. Cathleen dares to open one eye.

'They just want to keep you out of the way,' says the Doctor.

A few more of the zombie patients have moved into a position that cuts off your own avenues of escape. The three of you are backed into another corner of the room.

'Out of the way of what?' Amy wonders.

'Don't know,' confesses the Doctor, 'but I think we're about to find out.'

Some more of the zombies are moving towards the glass room.

'Ah,' whispers the Doctor and quickly he produces his sonic screwdriver. He points it in the direction of the door, which responds by sliding slowly back into place before any of the remote controlled patients can enter.

If the zombies use the keypad, go to 44.

If a new figure appears, go to 78.

'Only one way to be certain,' Amy says, with a determined glint in her eye. 'Come on, last one out's a loser.'

With that, she disappears into the whiteness that can be glimpsed through the half-open TARDIS door. You glance back at the Doctor who is looking around the room with a sad expression on his face.

'Don't worry,' he whispers. 'I'll soon have you back to normal.'

'I am normal,' you insist.

'I was talking to the ship,' the Doctor tells you and waves you through the door.

You step out into a vision of whiteness. As far as the eye can see there is snow and ice.

'Duck!' screams a familiar voice and instinctively you do as you are asked and duck down. A moment later something fast and white flies over your head.

SPLAT! You look up to see that a snowball has just exploded on the closing door of the TARDIS, showering the Doctor with snow as it falls apart.

'Hey!' For a moment you think the Doctor is angry and perhaps even hurt. He seems to be bent double. Is he in pain?

'Doctor?' Amy appears from the whiteness and takes a few steps towards the TARDIS.

Suddenly the Doctor springs upright and unleashes two snowballs simultaneously, one from each hand. The snowballs arc into the cold air and then crash into each other, directly above Amy, who is sprinkled with snow.

If you start a snow ball fight, go to 53.

If you see another spacecraft, go to 92.

The Sycorax completely ignores the Doctor and steps out through the door. A moment later, there is a flash of energy and a small explosion out in the corridor. You rush to the door to look out but the glass has become blackened. You stab a finger at the door control but nothing happens.

'He's locked us in,' you tell the others. 'I think he's broken the door!'

Amy sighs. 'So we're trapped!'

The Doctor is having none of it. 'Trapped? By a locked door, do me a favour.'

The Doctor starts pulling furniture away from the walls. 'Check every part of the wall,' he suggests, 'there must be another way out.'

You and Amy join the Doctor in a thorough examination of each of the walls and the floor of the room. Finally, you give up.

'It's no good,' you say, 'there is no other exit.'

The Doctor shakes his head. 'There is always an exit. We're breathing, aren't we? So there must be...'

'A ventilation shaft?'' suggests Amy. She grins at you. 'Like in the movies!'

'Exactly, but where is the access?' The Doctor scans the room again and then he spots it; a grille directly over the door. He grabs a table and pushes it across to the door. You all climb up to take a closer look. You can see that the grille is fixed into place with screws.

If the sonic screwdriver can unscrew them, go to 22.

If the sonic screwdriver can't unscrew them, go to 8.

The Doctor grabs the notebook and starts typing furiously. You ask him what he's doing, but he's too busy to answer.

'He's probably sending out for pizza,' says Amy, trying to lighten the mood.

'Hate pizza,' the Doctor mutters without slowing his typing speed for a moment.

He looks up at you and winks. 'Right, that should give me full access to the Sycorax ship's internal sensors. Now I can see if I can track down the energy signature of the creature...'

A three-dimensional map of the Sycorax Asteroid ship appears on the screen, with a bright glowing point representing the creature. 'There it is,' announces the Doctor. He stares at the screen intently for a moment then snaps the case shut and starts walking urgently towards one of the nearest passageways out of the chamber.

'Don't you need the map?' you ask him.

He points to his forehead, confidently. 'It's all up here,' he tells you.

Running to keep up, you and Amy follow him. As you move away from the large hollowed area where the engine was, you find yourselves in ever smaller tunnels. 'The Sycorax use creatures called Gagrinites to make these ships, you know,' the Doctor tells you, 'they're like little rhinos that eat rock.'

'It's like a maze in here,' you comment, as the pathways become narrower and darker. If it wasn't for the dim green glow of the sonic screwdriver, it would be very dark indeed.

The Doctor disappears around a corner.

Go to 99.

You go across to comfort the Doctor, but he is already getting to his feet.

'Come on then,' he suggests, 'lots to sort out yet.'

Over the next hour or two things get back to normal at the base. Cathleen, now no longer a Trainee Nurse after getting a field promotion from the base commander, is kept busy making sure that the recovering coma victims are all ready to report back to duty.

Meanwhile the Doctor makes a few adjustments to the Sycorax spaceship, powering down and neutralising the engines and wiping the computer core, much to Yasin's disappointment. 'No spoilers,' says the Doctor to him as explanation.

You and Amy find yourselves rather in the way and sneak off for a quick play in the snow. You borrow some of the base's cold weather gear and spend a happy half-hour playing snowballs and making the best snowmen ever.

Finally however, it is time to come in and when you get back inside the base the Doctor is waiting for you.

'I think it's time we slipped away,' says the Doctor. 'People are beginning to ask some awkward questions about who we are and where we come from.'

As you leave the changing rooms you notice something impossible; your name on the door.

'How is that possible?' you ask.

The Doctor takes a look and grins. 'This is the year 2024,' he tells you. 'Perhaps you've just seen a glimpse of *your* future...'

THE END

'That's the Cloister Bell,' the Doctor tells you. 'It's the ultimate alarm; it only sounds when things are really, really bad.'

'What things?' you ask, nervously.

The Doctor throws his arms up in the air and spins around.

'Everything,' he tells you, looking more than a little alarmed himself. 'Total systems failure. The TARDIS is dying.'

Amy takes a step towards him. 'What do you mean? Dying?'

The Doctor is now scampering around the console checking readings and running nervous hands through his hair while muttering to himself. He seems oblivious to you and Amy.

'Doctor!' Amy grabs him by the shoulder and he spins around.

'My ship is dying!' he shouts at her. 'Her power banks are being siphoned off. It's impossible, but it's happening.'

He turns back to the console.

'Only one thing we can do right now,' he announces. 'Hold on tight. Prepare for Emergency Materialisation.' With one hand the Doctor pulls down a lever on the console and you notice that his other hand is behind his back with his fingers crossed.

There is a sudden resounding boom and then everything is silent.

'Where have we landed?' asks Amy.

'Don't know, let's try and find out,' answers the Doctor activating a scanner from the console. The screen shows a flash of light and then goes blank. At the same time the lights begin to fade.

If Amy runs to the door, go to 28.

If the Doctor runs to the door, go to 60.

The Doctor tries to stop the Sycorax Warrior using his weapon but the massive creature just pushes past the Time Lord and brings down his crackling whip on to the surface of the liquid alien in the circular container.

There is a sudden flash of energy that lights up the room like a Roman candle and then the whip drops to the floor dead, as the Sycorax Warrior crumbles to dust.

'What happened?' you ask.

The Doctor pushes a hand through his hair and sighs sadly. 'Pretty much the same thing that happened to the crew of this base. This poor creature is a gentle space traveller called an Erali.'

'Gentle?' repeats Amy. 'It just killed the Sycorax thing.'

'In self-defence,' explains the Doctor. 'Just like the crew here. The Erali fell to Earth lost, hungry and scared and the scientists at this base found her, imprisoned her and experimented on her. They deserved everything that happened to them.'

You look at the creature with a mixture of fear and pity. 'So what happens now?'

'The Erali swim between the planets in the vacuum of space. They often go for hundreds or thousands of years between feeds so they have developed the means to store enormous amounts of energy. It's that facility to store energy that the scientists here wanted to understand.'

'So they're living batteries?' you suggest.

The Doctor nods. 'Trouble is, when the Sycorax ship and the TARDIS passed within range, the Erali rather over ate... Now it's got the worse case of wind in the history of the universe.'

'But is there any way to get the energy back from this Erali?' Amy wonders.

The Doctor frowns and then nods. 'I think so, but I'm going to have to help her. Time Lords have a great deal of control over our bodies. I need to merge with the Erali and show her how it's done. Keep back.'

To your amazement the Doctor turns and dives headfirst into the Erali's container, instantly disappearing beneath the pink liquid surface. The liquid begins to vibrate and bubble, and then there is a massive flash of intense white light that leaves you blinking and blinded.

When your eyes recover, there is no sign of the Erali and just the Doctor sitting cross-legged in the middle of the container she had been held in.

The Doctor gets to his feet. 'She's gone, back into Deep Space,' he tells you with a satisfied air.

'And what about the rest of the Sycorax?' demands Amy.

'They're powered up. Just like the TARDIS. When we get back to the surface I expect we'll find they too have disappeared. If they know what's good for them, they will. They don't want the Shadow Proclamation on their backs, do they?'

The Doctor looks around the room one more time and shakes his head, sadly. 'Time to go, I think.'

If you lead the way, go to 12.

If Amy leads the way, go to 55.

The Doctor tells you that it is a kind of spaceship.

'But it looks like a meteorite or something,' says Amy.

'It is,' agrees the Doctor, 'at least that's how it started out. But it's been made into a spaceship. It crashed here just like we did and not too long ago, I'd say.'

'So who drives a spaceship made of rock?' you wonder.

The Doctor pulls a face. 'Sycorax,' he says heavily.

'They sound... friendly,' speculates Amy, with more hope than certainty.

'Not really.' The Doctor frowns. 'I gave them a warning. Told them to stay away from this planet for good.'

'When was that?' you ask.

'Couple of Christmases back,' mutters the Doctor, deep in thought. 'A lifetime ago for me.'

You frown, unable to make sense of anything the Doctor is saying.

The Doctor is thinking fast. 'So first the TARDIS, then the Sycorax powered asteroid. Both drained of power, both here in the Antarctic wilderness. Why? What's the connection?'

'Whatever drained the TARDIS engines did the same to this flying rock?' suggests Amy.

The Doctor nods. 'Yes, yes, but why have we both landed here? It's too much of a coincidence.'

'Maybe whatever is behind it is right under our noses?' you speculate.

The Doctor whirls around. 'That's brilliant.' He spins round to address Amy, jabbing a finger in your direction. 'Brilliant humans sometimes, even the young ones.'

If Amy thinks she has an idea why you've been brilliant, go to 50.

If the Doctor tells you why you're brilliant, go to 83.

The voice you hear is Amy's.

'Hey,' she calls out. You walk out into a small ante-chamber and Amy is standing in front of you. 'Where did you get to?' she asks you.

A moment later another Amy appears from behind you. The new Amy grabs you by the arm and jerks you forwards, pushing past you as she does. You fall forwards, awkwardly and when you get to your feet the two Amys are standing side by side like a pair of identical twins.

Both the Amys point at each other and exclaim, 'She's the fake!' at the same time.

You look from one to another but there really isn't any way to tell them apart.

'This is just weird,' you mutter.

One of the Amys takes a step closer. 'Come on, it's me, you must know it's me.'

'I think we need the Doctor,' you tell her.

At that moment, to your great relief, you hear a very welcome sound coming from a direction up ahead.

'Hey, Amy what kept you?' It is the Doctor.

The Amy that held back suddenly jumps forwards, pushing you and her doppelgänger out of the way, before running off in the direction from which you heard the Doctor's voice.

'Is it really you?' you ask, helping the Amy that was pushed into you get back on her feet.

'Of course it's me,' she says, 'now come on, before its too late...'

She runs off after her double and you run after her.

Go to 99.

You take a closer look and see that the container appears to be full of some thick pinkish liquid. You reach out to see what it feels like and, to your astonishment, the liquid moves away from your hand to stop you touching it.

'It's alive!' you exclaim.

The Doctor hurries over to have a look. 'Oh, you poor thing,' he mutters when he sees the liquid creature. Gently he reaches out his hand. This time the liquid does not move away. Instead it flows towards the Doctor's hand and then up and over it, sticking closely to his skin. Like paint soaking into a paper towel the liquid seems to run up the Doctor's arm, over his shoulder and then towards his head.

'Doctor!' Amy calls out in alarm.

'Don't panic,' insists the Doctor, 'I'm perfectly safe,' A moment later the liquid rolls over his face and his head and then he is completely enveloped in the pink liquid. A second later and the liquid retreats, leaving the Doctor without a mark on him.

'Amazing,' says the Doctor. 'Telepathy through physical contact.'

'What did you find out?' asks Amy.

'Well I know where all the energy went,' the Doctor tells you, 'and how we can get it back.'

Before he can say any more, the door bursts open and the Sycorax Warrior appears, his whip in his hand ready to strike.

If the Doctor stops him in time, go to 35.

If the Doctor doesn't reach him in time, go to 67.

The Doctor jumps to his feet.

'Problem is you never allowed for the possibility of spaceships passing by your energy scoop, did you? Now you lot,' the Doctor points at the lone Sycorax, 'is your asteroid powered by an All Speed Inter-System Type K Engine, as usual?'

'A K2,' the Sycorax clarifies.

The Doctor blows out his cheeks. 'A K2? Well that gives us a mountain to climb.' He stops for a moment and looks around the room. 'Anyone? Never mind. Right, so you've got all that K2 fission energy plus a stack load of artron energy from my ship which all adds up to a lot more energy than you bargained for.'

And now he is pointing back towards the Professor.

'So you've got this great big energy hoover and you've just sucked up enough energy to power the sun for a couple of millennium. Result – the second biggest bang in history unless we do something right now.'

'Destroy the machine.' insists the Sycorax.

'No!' shouts the Doctor. 'That will kill us all and take out half this solar system at the same time.'

'There must be something you can do?' you wonder. 'If only this machine had never been switched on in the first place.'

The Doctor grabs you by the shoulders. 'That's it!' he cries out, 'I knew you were smart.'

'I am?' you say.

The Doctor is nodding. 'We need to turn back time.'

If the Sycorax attacks anyway, go to 87.

If the Doctor carries out his idea, go to 33.

The creature begins to blur and change. In seconds he changes from looking like the Sycorax leader to being a grey humanoid with plain features and deep blue eyes.

'I will do as you ask,' he tells the Doctor, 'but can you guarantee that I will not be their captive again?'

'I promise you as a Time Lord of Gallifrey,' the Doctor tells him, solemnly.

The shape-shifter nods. 'In that case, I will send the energy I stole back to where it came from. Without any great fuss the grey alien begins to glow with a pulsating yellow light. Slowly the Sycorax engines behind him begin to show signs of life as their energy cells are replenished.

Finally the process comes to an end and the alien staggers with the sudden weakness. Without warning the Sycorax Leader suddenly launches an attack. Pushing the Doctor out of the way, he lunges forwards with his energy whip, spearing it into the shape-shifter's stomach.

Wild blue electricity leaps and bounces all over the alien's body but then it spreads back along the handle of the whip and covers the Sycorax Leader. The two aliens jerk and spasm as the terrible energies course all over their bodies before, finally, they both fall to the floor and stop twitching. The Doctor nudges the lifeless body of the Sycorax Leader, then hurries across to the shape-shifter, but it is too late – he is also dead.

If you go to the Doctor, go to 65.

If Amy goes to the Doctor, go to 76.

You type in the letters: "WILLIAMS" on the screen and some data appears, but it's all jumbled-up letters.

'It's some kind of corrupted file,' suggests Amy.

'That keeps happening recently,' Cathleen tells you.

'Really,' comments the Doctor, 'that's interesting...'

He gets out his sonic screwdriver and after carefully adjusting the settings he gives the computer a quick blast. On the screen the jumbled-up letters rearrange themselves into legible English.

The Doctor starts reading at an incredible speed, flicking from page to page before you can even read a few words. After speed-reading what looked to be about twenty pages of text, he spins around in his chair.

'Well they all fell into a coma,' he tells you.

'We knew that!' retorts Amy.

'But the interesting thing is, that shortly before this all happened, there was a security alert. There was a theft in the base. Right?' He is looking at Cathleen, who nods.

'It was really weird,' she confirms, 'someone stole something from sick bay.'

'But not medicines or drugs,' the Doctor continues the story, 'blood.'

'Blood samples of all members of staff are kept in case of medical need,' Cathleen explains.

'So what would anyone want with those blood samples?' asks Amy.

Suddenly you hear sounds of movement. When you turn around you see that every patient is sitting bolt upright. Now, in eerie unison, they swing their legs out of bed. A moment later they are on their feet and staggering, zombie-style, towards you.

If you are trapped, go to 18.

If you can reach the door, go to 39.

74

'No!' shouts the Doctor but it is too late. The body of the Sycorax Warrior, lit up with blue lightning, suddenly falls to the floor, and lies deathly still. The Doctor hurries over to it and checks for a pulse. He shakes his head, sadly. 'He wouldn't be told,' he mutters to himself.

Behind him the machinery is still glowing dangerously.

'Doctor?' you try to get his attention.

The Doctor looks up and seems to remember what was going on. 'Right, of course, things to be done.' He jumps to his feet and starts working at one of the computer consoles again.

'Thing with energy is it's difficult to store and difficult to transmit,' he tells you, while his fingers skip over the keyboard in a blur, 'but we're got one thing on our side – time.'

'I thought you said we didn't have much time?' Amy says.

The Doctor flashes you a quick grin. 'Artron energy,' he tells you mysteriously, 'time energy from a time ship. Handled by someone with the right qualifications – that'd be me, by the way – we've got all the time in the world.'

The Doctor presses the entry key and suddenly everything goes very strange. The air feels thick as if it has turned into invisible jelly and everything looks a little blurry as if you were looking at things through a heat haze. Every moment, every minute, seems to be in slow motion. With the exception of one thing – the Doctor, striding towards you though the slow time at normal speed. He grabs you and Amy and the Professor and pulls you all into a group hug.

'You need an anchor,' he tells you, speaking normally.

'W – h – a – t ?' you ask and your voice comes out so slowly that the word seems to take a minute to say.

'A time sensitive, like me, to anchor you against the time tide. I've dropped a very big stone into this lake of time and I don't want any of you washed away by the ripples,' the Doctor tells you.

And then, as suddenly as it started, it is all over. Normality pops back into existence but now all the machinery has gone, as has the body of the Sycorax Warrior.

'What happened?' asks the Professor, 'Where's my lab equipment?'

'Gone,' says the Doctor. 'In fact it was never here, like the aliens and their asteroid spaceship. There's been a contained temporal schism.' He grins wildly. 'Like a reset button on a video game.'

'So the Sycorax ship never lost power and never crashed?' you ask.

'Exactly.'

'But what about us? If there was no power drain why are we here?' you wonder.

The Doctor grins. 'That is what we call a time paradox.'

The Professor is wide-eyed at all of this. 'Time,' he mutters to himself, and wanders off.

The Doctor suddenly slaps his forehead. 'Professor Howkins, of course. I should have remembered the name. In 2025 he publishes some of humankind's first tentative steps towards a unified theory of time having shifted from his original studies of new energy sources for mysterious reasons...'

'Guess they're not so mysterious now, eh?' says Amy smiling.

'Guess not,' the Doctor agrees before looking at you. 'Now talking about time, I guess it's time we got you home. Come on, back to the TARDIS...'

THE END

75

There is a deafening BOOM and then all is silent.

After a moment you open your eyes and find that the glass room has completely shattered. The scaffolding is in pieces and the soap bubble micro-universe has disappeared.

Amy helps you to your feet. The Doctor is already out in the room checking on the recovering crew members.

'They're free of the Sycorax control,' he announces after examining a couple of the patients. 'Should be right as rain in a few minutes.'

The Doctor seeks out the base commander and asks her a few questions.

A short while later he comes back to you and Amy and beckons you to follow him. You realise that he is leading you back to the TARDIS.

'Best if we just slip away,' he says.

'But what happened?' you ask.

Amy hazards a guess. 'That thief crashed here in a spaceship, right? And that's when your UNIT friends got involved...'

The Doctor nods. 'UNIT brought the crash remains here and populated this base with experts to study it.'

'And the shape-shifter?'

'My guess is that she was injured in the crash, hid and laid low until she could figure out a way to get off planet,' the Doctor tells you. 'But then the micro-universe drained the TARDIS energy banks and suddenly it was a different ball game.'

You arrive at the TARDIS. The Doctor grins, seeing it lit up as usual and making its normal slight humming sound.

'In you go,' says the Doctor, opening the door. 'Let's get you home.'

THE END.

Amy goes to the Doctor and puts a comforting arm round his shoulder. It is clear that the adventure is over.

The Doctor spends the next hour or two sorting out a few details. He powers down the Sycorax ship and, much to Yasin's horror, he wipes the ship's computer memory. 'You'll have plenty to do retro engineering these space engines,' the Doctor tells him, 'I can't make it too easy for you.'

The rest of the crew, released from their Sycorax-induced coma, are making a full recovery under the care of Nurse Cathleen, whose field promotion is the first act by the commander when she finds out what has been happening.

Yasin is trying to persuade the Doctor to stay and help him with his work. Amy comes over to you and beckons you to join her.

'Doctor,' she says, 'Won't you need to get your tool kit, if you're going to help?'

'My tool kit?' The Doctor frowns.

'Yes, the one you keep in your blue storage box,' says Amy and both you and the Doctor cotton on to what she is suggesting.

'Oh, *that* tool kit,' says the Doctor, 'yes, let's go and get it.'

'I know where it is,' you say, joining in the fun.

The three of you almost run back towards the place where you left the TARDIS, leaving Cathleen and Yasin shaking their heads.

The Doctor grins as the three of you enter the TARDIS, 'Time to go home.'

THE END

The Doctor leads the way down the right-hand corridor. The floor is slightly at an angle because the ship is not level, but even with this you soon notice that the corridor is taking you down into the heart of the ship. After a few minutes walking you still have not encountered any crew.

'It's like a ghost ship,' you comment.

'It's a mostly automated ship,' the Doctor tells you. 'It might only have a crew of three or four people.'

You find yourself shivering. 'Something doesn't feel right,' you say, 'it's bright and light but still spooky.'

'I know what you mean,' agrees Amy and she squeezes your arm gently.

'Maybe whatever sucked the energy out of the TARDIS is in here somewhere...' you suggest.

The Doctor shrugs. 'Maybe...'

The Doctor comes to a sudden stop and you and Amy walk right into him.

'Sorry,' he says and steps to one side so you can see what caused him to stop. You've reached a massive thick bulkhead door that is preventing you from going further.

There is a glass viewing panel in the middle of the door, but it is totally opaque and impossible to see anything through. There is a numeric keypad set into the door.

'Often these things are left with the factory settings,' the Doctor suggests. 'Try 7890.'

If you have access to a computer, click on box B on screen and enter the code 7890.

If you do not, go to 20.

The Doctor is still holding his sonic screwdriver, but a moment later, there is a flash of movement and it is knocked from his hand by some kind of energy whip.

You turn around and see a giant alien warrior is wielding the whip. He is dressed in a red cloak and wears a belt that seems to be decorated with bones and shanks of hair. Although humanoid, he is clearly not human. His head is all inside out with a big bony exo-skeleton covering a face that appears to be all exposed muscle. It reminds you of cut-away pictures of the human body that you've seen in a book where the skin has been removed so you can see how various bits work.

'I was wondering when you'd show up,' comments the Doctor, waggling his fingers where the sonic screwdriver was snatched. 'This is a Sycorax!' he continues. 'The puppet master behind our friends in the coma. The old blood control thing...'

The Sycorax opens its mouth, which is filled with sharp fangs, and says something in its raw guttural language.

'Sorry mate, don't speak Sycorax that well.'

'I said do not interfere,' says the nearest zombie suddenly.

The Doctor's eyes widen. 'Oh, that's clever.'

'I am not here to impress your inferior species,' says the alien, through the patient's mouth. 'I am here for my prize.'

If he explains what his prize is, go to 10.

If the Doctor guesses what his prize is, go to 86.

79

The Doctor tries the door and finds that it opens easily.

'That's odd, isn't it?' you say, following the Doctor inside.

'Not really,' the Doctor says, 'why lock your door when there's no one for miles around?'

Inside the plastic igloo there is a small airlock and when you have passed through this you find yourself in a lobby containing the top of a lift shaft with shiny metal doors, just like you'd see in a multi-storey car park. The igloo itself is made from curved sheets of plastic, bonded together with plastic screws; it's clearly just a shelter for the lift entrance to the base below. Beyond the airlock the air is heated and, seeing some pegs, you all remove your snowsuits and hang them up.

'Right, let's explore,' says the Doctor.

There is just one button on a panel next to the lift doors and it shows an arrow pointing down.

The Doctor jabs at it and a rumbling noise starts up as the lift begins to rise up from the bottom of the shaft. A moment later the lift cage arrives and the metallic doors slide open.

The Doctor leads the way into the lift. 'Guess the only way is down,' comments Amy, as the doors slide shut again. A moment later the lift begins to descend. It seems to take a long time, but finally the lift stops moving.

If the doors open automatically, go to 26.

If the doors stay closed, go to 42.

80

The glass is opaque and smoky. The Doctor tries to take a closer look but even with his face pressed up against the glass he can't make out anything inside.

'Do you know what's in here?' he asks Cathleen.

The trainee nurse just shrugs. 'No idea,' she confesses, 'except that it's really important.'

The Doctor takes out his sonic screwdriver and begins waving it in the air, as if trying to measure something in the atmosphere with it. It makes a quiet whistling noise which changes pitch as it gets closer to the glass room.

'There's definitely a trace of artron energy here,' he says out loud.

You take a look at Amy, who just shrugs. 'Is that the energy stolen from the TARDIS?' you guess. To your delight the Doctor immediately begins to nod. 'Time energy, very dangerous stuff in the wrong hands and this is very definitely wrong.'

He walks around the glass room, looking for the door, and finally comes across it on the far side.

'Does this door have a key?' he asks.

Cathleen laughs. 'You're a bit twentieth century aren't you? Keys? It's all access codes here.'

'So what's the code?' asks Amy, seeing the Doctor getting annoyed.

'I'm not sure,' Cathleen tells you. But you could try 000,' she suggests. 'Some of the scientists find it hard to remember lots of different PINs and end up resetting everything to that.'

If you have access to a computer, click on box E on screen and enter the code 000.

If you do not, go to 56.

'I don't have it,' you tell the Doctor. He stops and stares at you, brushing his floppy fringe of hair out of his eyes absentmindedly.

'No, he gave it to me,' the pretty red-headed girl tells him, handing over the screwdriver that you gave her just a moment before. The strange pair had appeared in your street and asked you for a screwdriver. Luckily you remembered seeing one at home and had hurriedly fetched it. When you had returned to the strangers, the girl had taken the tool with a quick thank you and dashed off with the man she called "Doctor."

You had followed them into an alley where you watched with astonishment as they disappeared into a large blue box that was labelled a "police box", whatever that was meant to be.

You had followed them through the doors and found yourself in this impossible room.

You watch as the Doctor takes the screwdriver and fiddles with something on the mushroom-shaped central console.

The red-headed girl takes a step towards you and smiles reassuringly. 'I'm Amy,' she tells you. 'And that's the Doctor. And this, is a space and time machine called the TARDIS.'

'It can go anywhere in space and time,' says the Doctor. 'Into the distant past or the far future.'

'And have you back in time for tea,' adds Amy, 'if you're lucky!'

If you ask to go back in time, go to 97.

If you don't believe her, go to 24.

The dialogue box at the bottom of the screen remains blank as the Sycorax takes a long moment to think.

'Come on, don't be shy,' the Doctor encourages him. 'If you explain I can help.'

'I need the humans to hunt for the D**&HO&,' the alien tells you.

'I think the machine just broke,' you say.

The Doctor shakes his head. 'Software can only translate common words, not proper names,' he points out. 'What was that again? A Kriftlok?' The Doctor somehow manages to pronounce the alien name with the same guttural tone as the Sycorax did.

The Sycorax nods. 'It is a fearful creature.'

Amy and you exchange a worried look. What kind of monster would be bad enough for this alien to think it fearful?

'Look, you don't need slave humans. Let them go and I will help you myself. One of me is worth a dozen zombies any day of the week.' The Sycorax hesitates again.

'Just tell me more about this Kriftlok,' the Doctor asks him.

'It is a beast, an animal. It has no intelligence and it is very dangerous. It feeds on energy which it can store inside its body.'

'Where did it come from?' you wonder.

'We found it lying dormant and abandoned by its swarm and realised that many would pay handsomely for such a creature,' says the Sycorax, 'so we took it aboard our craft.'

If the Sycorax continues his story, go to 84.

If something interrupts him, go to 41.

'What did I say?' you ask.

The Doctor drops to his knees and begins digging with his gloved hands, sending showers of snow behind him, like a human-shaped digging machine.

'You said the answer was right under our noses, didn't you?' he asks, 'and you were right. In fact it's right under our feet.'

You peer into the hole he has made and see something that is not white at the bottom. The Doctor leans into the hole and raps the dark grey surface he has uncovered.

CLANG!

'It's metal!' you cry out.

The Doctor looks at you and grins.

'There's something down there, some kind of construct,' he tells you, his eyes bright with excitement.

From somewhere within his special parka he produces his sonic screwdriver and scans the area.

'Whatever it is,' he announces, 'it's quite big.'

'Could it be another spaceship?' you wonder.

The Doctor gets to his feet, still scanning with the sonic screwdriver.

'Might be,' he answers you, 'but it's looking more like some kind of base. An underground Antarctic base. Exciting, isn't it?'

He starts moving off, scanning with the sonic screwdriver the whole time. Suddenly he cries out, 'Ah!'

You and Amy run to join him. In the whiteness, the Doctor has found a small hump of what looks like snow. You touch it and realise that it's some kind of plastic with an almost invisible door set into it.

If the door is locked, go to 48.

If the door is unlocked, go to 79.

The Sycorax continues his story, his rough guttural language translated, almost instantaneously, into typed English by the netbook-like device.

'We were passing this dirtball planet when the creature suddenly revived itself. Its hunger was unstoppable, it drained our engines causing us to crash here in this ice. The rest, you know.'

The Doctor nods, taking all of this in. 'And where are you now?'

'The beast has us trapped in a far part of the asteroid ship, close to the sleeping halls,' the Sycorax leader explains. 'It has collapsed tunnels and created chaos. We are completely cut off. That is why I needed the humans – to dig us out.'

'And where is the beast?' asks Amy.

'I don't know,' says the Sycorax simply, 'but there is something else you should know. It is a shape-shifter. And although it is a beast, it has a certain wild intelligence. It can mimic other creatures perfectly.'

'How do we know we're not talking to it right now?' asks Amy.

The alien's red eyes narrow in fury. 'Sycorax do not lie.'

The Doctor pushes Amy out of the way and addresses the Sycorax.

'Okay, here's the deal. I'll find this creature, reverse the power drain and repair your engines. In return, you leave this planet and never come back. Deal?'

The Sycorax looks very unhappy at the idea of making a deal with an inferior species, but eventually he agrees.

If the Doctor needs to use the netbook some more, go to 64.

If he sets off into the caves, go to 93.

The Sycorax Warrior considers for a long moment and then nods.

'Fellow victims. Agreed. We will work together to find those responsible for attacking us both. Then we will kill them.'

The Doctor shakes his head. 'Or perhaps we can just have a quiet word, eh. We don't know for certain if there was an intent to attack our ships. It may have been... accidental.'

The Sycorax Warrior refuses to respond to this suggestion. 'Sycorax scanners located source of power drain in this complex. We need to find source. Sycorax Rock.'

'What's that? Is the name of his space ship *Sycorax Rock?*' Amy mutters to the Doctor, but not quietly enough not to be heard and translated by the alien's necklace.

'Sycorax Rock,' echoes the alien, approvingly.

'Sycorax Rock,' you add, joining in the fun.

'He thinks you're his fan club now,' the Doctor tells you both.

The alien leads you back out into the corridor and walks off at speed. You have to almost run to keep up with him.

'What is he?' you whisper to the Doctor.

'Alien race of scavengers and chancers called the Sycorax,' he tells you. 'Scientifically advanced, but they prefer to dress it up with a bit of voodoo.'

'Friendly?' you whisper back.

The Doctor shakes his head very slightly.

The alien reaches a door and pulls it open, savagely.

The room beyond is a large laboratory filled with strange-looking machinery.

If there is a man there, go to 36.

If the room is empty, go to 90.

'You're after the thing in that room,' says the Doctor. 'Am I right?'

The Sycorax nods.

'But you don't even know what it is!' screams the Doctor.

'What it is, is mine!' insists the Sycorax. 'Stolen from my own ship by a deceitful thief, a Yarkop.'

'Shape-shifters,' says the Doctor. 'Yeah, I've met Yarkops. But they're not that bad. Bit dim maybe, but there's a lot of that about.'

'The Yarkop took my prize and ran,' the alien continues, still being translated by the coma patient... we chased it through five systems until it took to ground here on this pathetic mudball.'

'Which was a bit of a problem for you,' suggests the Doctor, 'cos you lot are forbidden from stepping foot on planet Earth, aren't you?'

He turns to you and Amy and gives you a sly wink. 'Can't imagine how that came to happen,' he whispers. Calmly, he bends over and retrieves his sonic screwdriver from the floor.

'I teleported in alone,' says the Sycorax Warrior. 'I needed slaves to help me locate the device. Now I can take it and go.'

'Trouble is, it's not that simple,' the Doctor tells him, sauntering into the middle of the room. 'That's not your property or the Yarkop's, is it? That was made by the WarpWeavers of Blue Halo Alpha. They're the only race with the skill to make constructs with interdimensional

reality warping. One false move with that and we'll all be history.'
 'You're bluffing,' responds the Sycorax.

Go to 14.

The Sycorax Warrior runs into the centre of the room and begins wielding his whip. It swishes around in the air, crackling with energy and THWACK! It connects with some of the machinery. The machinery glows yellow and blue and then disintegrates into powder.

'No!' screams the Professor. 'You don't know what you're doing.'

He begins to run towards the alien, but Amy restrains him and you rush to help.

'Don't try and stop him,' you tell the Professor, 'he'll just try and use that thing on you.'

The Sycorax has moved on to attack more and more of the energy-draining machinery. The Doctor looks around the scene of utter destruction with concern written all over his face. 'This is not good,' he mutters almost to himself.

Quickly he points his sonic screwdriver towards the ceiling and sets off the fire sprinklers. The water hits the whip and shorts it out. It fizzes uselessly and flails against machinery without having any effect.

Enraged, the Sycorax roars in anger and picks up the nearest computer. He throws it into the energy drainer and there is a terrible flash of blue light.

You cover your eyes with your hand and when you are able to look again, you see that the Sycorax is shuddering and shaking in what looks like a haze of blue electricity running all over his body.

If the Sycorax falls to the floor, go to 74.

If the Doctor saves him, go to 38.

Taking a deep breath, you walk over to the double doors and step out into the icy wasteland.

Amy's description didn't prepare you for the amazing sight that greets you. You are grateful for the goggles that the Doctor provided you with because even through the tinted lenses the view is dazzlingly bright. It is the snowiest snow scene you have ever seen. It is like a desert of white sand. You take a few steps out into the wilderness, watching your booted feet crunching footprints into the previously untouched snow.

You glance back at the TARDIS and can't help but be amused at the strange sight of the bright blue police box – the only object in colour for miles around – standing proudly in the snow.

Amy and the Doctor emerge from the TARDIS and share the view. The Doctor closes the door behind him and pats it with a gloved hand.

'Don't worry,' you hear him whisper, 'we'll get you back to normal.'

As he steps away from the doors the last of the light from inside fades to black and the constant background hum of the TARDIS is silenced.

'Watch out!' shouts Amy suddenly. You spin around and see that Amy has gathered up a snowball which she launches into the air. You duck and the snowball sails over your head, hitting the TARDIS and sending a shower of snow over you.

If you start a snowball fight, go to 53.

If you see something unusual, go to 92.

The Sycorax stops, but does not immediately turn back.

'Please, listen to me,' says the Doctor. 'Violence is not the answer. There's mystery here, but together we can get to the bottom of it.'

Now the Sycorax does turn around, his red angry eyes just narrow slits, burning beneath his bony forehead. 'Sycorax do not need help from humans,' he insists and then he turns again, his long red cloak swishing across the powdery top layer of snow.

You watch as the frightening-looking aliens march off across the snow.

The Doctor shakes his head, disappointed.

'Who are the Sycorax then?'   asks Amy. 'Weren't they in a Shakespeare play?'

The Doctor laughs. 'Sort of. That was my fault. I kinda gave Will the name. But it belonged to this lot first. Intergalactic scavengers. They make nothing themselves, just steal from others. '

'Like the Wombles?' says Amy.

'Yeah but nowhere near as cuddly. Sycorax are nasty, violent and a bit obsessed with ritual and voodoo. And if that base is manned there'll be a blood bath.'

'Can't you do something? Call for help?' you wonder.

The Doctor spins around, waving his hands at the wilderness that surrounds you. 'We're miles from anywhere. No, we're going to have to sort this out ourselves.'

'The three of us? Against that lot?' Amy doesn't sound convinced.

'The Sycorax won't be a problem if we can solve the energy loss,' the Doctor tells you.

If Amy sees something, go to 6.

If you see something, go to 34.

You follow the Sycorax Warrior into the room. The Doctor picks up a mug and sniffs its contents. 'Coffee,' he tells you. 'About two days old.'

'How can you tell that?' asks Amy.

The Doctor points at his face. 'Very good nose on this body. Actually I've always been lucky with noses. Although some of mine have been a bit on the large side. Still, you can't pick your own nose, can you?' He laughs, enjoying his own joke, but the Sycorax Warrior is not amused. He slams down his fist on a desk, sending papers and pens flying.

'Where is source of energy drain?' says the electronic voice translating his words almost instantaneously. 'I will call my brothers to join me and we will tear this place apart.'

'No, no wait,' the Doctor implores him. 'Give me some time. Let's not go all Judoon on this.'

The Sycorax snorts at the Doctor's mention of the Judoon – whoever they are. 'Ha! Judoon are fools,' the Sycorax says, clearly amused, 'but make tasty meal and hide good for wearing.'

Amy has found a computer, which is working. 'I wonder if this can tell us anything?'

The Doctor hurries over to take a look.

'We need the user password to access the data,' he mutters.

You see a scribbled word pinned to a board above the desk: SNOWMAN.

'How about that?' you suggest jabbing a finger at the word.

If you have access to a computer, click on box C on screen and enter the code word SNOWMAN.

If you do not, go to 4.

It is Amy. She appears from out of one of the many tunnels that meet in this little chamber.

'I've found it,' she tells you and starts hurrying back the way she came. 'Come on!'

You start to follow her, but the Doctor holds you back.

'Wait,' he orders you. A moment later there is a small explosion and the roof of the tunnel you were about to run into collapses in a rush of rock debris and dust.

'That wasn't Amy!' you realise.

'I thought we were hunting the creature,' the Doctor comments, 'but it looks like it has been hunting us.'

'What should we do?' you ask the Doctor.

'We go back,' the Doctor tells you. 'Double speed. If the fake Amy gets back before we do, we'll be in a right pickle.'

Hurrying back the way you have just come proves to be quite difficult. Viewed from the opposite direction it feels like unfamiliar territory again and seems to take even longer than the first time.

Finally, however, you get back to the chamber containing the Sycroax's engines.

Amy and Cathleen are there with Yasin. All three are cowering against a wall keeping well clear of two figures that are circling each other – two identical Sycorax Leaders. One has an energy whip in his hands, apart from that one detail they appear to be perfect copies of each other.

If the Doctor runs between them, go to 58.

If the Doctor hesitates, go to 49.

Amy launches another snowball and you duck behind the TARDIS to take cover.

You see something that had previously been hidden from view behind the space-time ship — some large object a hundred metres or so away. It looks like a chunk of rock but, bizarrely, it does not have any snow on it at all, making it look totally out of place.

'Hey, come and look at this,' you shout out and a moment later the Doctor and Amy join you.

'Wow!' says Amy, impressed.

'Let's take a closer look,' you suggest.

You start running towards the rock and, as you get closer, you realise that it is even larger than you first realised. When you reach it, the side of the thing towers over you like a cliff at the seaside. To your surprise the rock is warm to the touch and you can see where it has begun to melt the surface ice where it has landed.

'Why is this rock warm?' you wonder.

'Because it's not a rock,' the Doctor tells you, as he joins you in examining the object.

'Well, it looks like a rock, it feels like a rock, how come it isn't?' asks Amy.

The Doctor is looking around him, with a nervous expression on his face.

'What are you looking for, Doctor?' you wonder.

'Crew,' he mutters. 'There must have been some.'

'What?'

If you hear a new voice, go to 17.

If the Doctor explains the rock, go to 68.

Without another word the Doctor heads off for the nearest tunnel. Amy and you have to run to catch up with him.

'I can track the energy spillage from the creature with the sonic screwdriver,' the Doctor tells you. 'It should lead us straight to him.'

'Great!' says Amy.

The rocky passageway that you are walking along is smoother than you would have expected.

'Are these tunnels natural?' you wonder.

The Doctor shakes his head. 'The asteroids are almost hollowed out to make the Sycorax spaceships,' he explains. 'Where they come from on Fire Trap there is an indigenous rock-eating worm that they use to make their ships.'

As you walk deeper into the system of tunnels it becomes darker and colder. For the first time since you landed, you can believe that you really are in the Antarctic. The tunnels all seem to weave and intercut with each other, forming a complex maze.

'Don't go too quickly, Doctor,' says Amy, voicing your own concerns. 'If we lose you, we might never find the way out again.'

'Don't worry,' the Doctor assures you, 'I'm not going to leave you.'

Suddenly there is an almighty animal roar from somewhere up ahead.

Despite his promise the Doctor starts to run. Reluctantly, you and Amy break into a run to try and keep up with him again.

Go to 99.

The Sycorax stops in the doorway. 'The reason for my ship's loss of power is in this Lab 3. I will deal with it. Our alliance is at an end,' he tells you, before going though the door and then there is a flash of light as his whip destroys the door control.

The Doctor runs across to the door and tries to open it but it is sealed tight.

'He's locked us in,' he announces.

'We're trapped?' you ask.

The Doctor shakes his head. 'Takes more than a locked door to trap me.'

'Sonic?' suggests Amy.

'Not this time,' the Doctor tells her, scurrying around the room looking for another way out. 'Thing is, this kind of base in the middle of nowhere... very difficult to get bricks and the like.'

He is now on his hands and knees looking at where the walls meet the floor.

'So the whole thing gets made elsewhere and put together here like a giant kit,' continues the Doctor. 'And each wall section can have more than one use; for example, you may get a section like this which is unbroken, while other sections have windows, doors or hatches cut into them. Like this one.'

He is back on his feet and pulling some filing cabinets away from the wall. Behind them, you can see that there is a rectangular panel set into the wall at head height. The panel has a cover secured by screws.

If the sonic screwdriver can't unscrew them, go to 8.

If the sonic screwdriver can unscrew them, go to 22.

The voice belongs to Trainee Nurse Cathleen. She comes staggering out of one of the many tunnels that meet at this point, looking pale and quite beside herself with fear.

'We've found it,' she manages to tell you, her voice shaking with fear. 'This way, come quick.'

She turns on her heel and disappears back into the tunnel she just emerged from. The Doctor moves to follow her.

'Doctor, wait!' you cry out. 'Could that have been the shape-shifter?'

The Doctor turns to look at you and pulls a face, wide-eyed and a little taken aback. 'Well, it could be. Maybe we should catch her up and ask her.' As he turns back to carry on following her, there is a sudden flash in the tunnel and a section of the roof comes tumbling down, just in front of the Doctor. A cloud of dust is sent into the air.

You help the Doctor stagger back, away from the debris.

'You were right, thanks,' says the Doctor.

'So what do we do now?' you wonder.

'We need to get back to the others,' the Doctor says.

When you get back to the engine chamber you immediately see Amy, Cathleen and Yasin cowering on the far wall, trying to keep out of the way of two imposing figures who are circling each other slowly in the middle of the room; two almost identical Sycorax Leaders.

If the Doctor runs between them, go to 58.

If the Doctor hesitates, go to 49.

The Sycorax ignore the Doctor and keep walking away over the ice. Their long cloaks brush the soft powdery top layer of snow behind them like built-in brooms. With the slight breeze blowing up puffs of the snow all the time, there is soon little to be seen of the alien footsteps in the snow. The red figures quickly become just dots on the horizon and then they are gone.

The Doctor watches them go, deep in thought.

'Who are that lot, then?' you ask finally, unable to contain your question any more.

'A rather nasty bunch of intergalactic scavengers. They don't make anything themselves, they just take things other people make. They don't even make spaceships; they just find suitable asteroids, hollow them out and strap ugly great spaceship engines to them.'

'So they recycle, that's good isn't it?' you say.

The Doctor shakes his head. 'Not the way the Sycorax do it. They're a violent lot. They like to use coercion, threats, blackmail, and they wrap their science up with a lot of mystical mumbo-jumbo, all voodoo rituals and blood rites. Not my kind of aliens at all!'

'So what will they do when they get to the research base?'

The Doctor looks grim. 'Nothing good. There's only one way to stop them. We have to discover what caused that energy drain and find a way to reverse it,' the Doctor announces. 'If we can repower their ship, the Sycorax can leave.'

If Amy sees something, go to 6.

If you see something, go to 34.

'You mean you can actually travel in time? Can you take me to the past?' You realise that you are gabbling in your excitement and force yourself to stop talking so that the Doctor can answer you.

'Let me guess, you want to see dinosaurs?' He turns to look at Amy. 'They always want to see dinosaurs. I blame *Jurassic Park*.'

'I'm not bothered about dinosaurs,' you say, worried now that the Doctor will say no. 'I just like history. I'm interested in how people used to live, that kind of thing.'

The Doctor's face lights up. 'Interested in people? Me too.' He gives you back the screwdriver, which you slip into a pocket. He sees the expression on your face and offers an explanation.

'Some of the fixtures on the console are, well, not exactly the original design specs and my trusty sonic screwdriver doesn't have a setting for them,' explains the Doctor.

'Sonic screwdriver?' You wonder what on earth he can mean.

The Doctor produces a slim green-tipped metal tool from his jacket pocket. 'This is the sonic screwdriver,' he tells you.

'It's a bit like a Swiss Army Knife with added tech,' Amy informs you, more helpfully.

The Doctor shoots her a look and then continues, ignoring her interruption.

'Anyway, thanks to you, I've been able to recalibrate the temporal drift circuits and we're all systems go again, ready for take off.'

'This box flies?' you ask.

'Amongst other things,' the Doctor answers you with a big grin. 'Fancy a quick trip, then?'

If you say yes, go to 9.

If you hesitate, go to 40.

You and the Doctor take the tunnel to the left and soon find yourselves going deep into the heart of the Sycorax ship.

'These tunnels aren't natural, you know,' the Doctor tells you, as you walk deeper and deeper into the increasing darkness. 'The Sycorax bore out all these tunnels by hand, creating a nest of artificial caves linked by passageways. They even have them open to the surface and use forcefields to maintain atmospheric pressure.

'Why have holes to the surface?' you wonder.

'They're big on things like sunlight and starlight, appeals to their weird sense of mysticism,' the Doctor explains. 'Makes for some of the most peculiar spaceships you'll ever see.'

The Doctor consults his sonic screwdriver again. 'The energy signal is going off the scale,' he tells you. 'And we're very close now...'

A moment or two later you stumble out of the narrow tunnel that you are in and find yourselves in another large chamber. Looking up you can see lots and lots of recesses joined by narrow walkways disappearing above you.

'The Sycorax cryogenic facility,' announces the Doctor. 'It might look like ancient graves, but these are actually state-of-the-art cryogenic suspended animation cells. The rock is a great conductor of the exceptionally low temperatures needed to freeze a living creature.'

You realise that it is very cold in here, like when you walk past the frozen food section in the supermarket, but much, much worse.

'Hey!' someone cries.

If it is Amy, go to 91.

If it is Nurse Cathleen, go to 95.

You and Amy hurry around the next corner and find yourself face to face with two identical Doctors.

'I think we've found him,' says the first Doctor, who is standing closest to you.

'He's a very good shape-shifter and mimic,' says the second Doctor, who is standing nearest to Amy.

You and Amy exchange looks. Which of these is the real Doctor?

'What year in the past did you take me to first?' asks Amy, as a test.

The Doctor standing closest to Amy shakes his head sadly. 'It's no good asking test questions like that – the creature is telepathic, it can read my mind,' he tells Amy.

'Look we haven't got time for this,' insists "your" Doctor, 'we need to get the energy back into the ships.'

'Without that energy I will be weak,' the second Doctor tells you, revealing himself to be the fake. 'The Sycorax will enslave me.'

The Doctor reaches out to his double. 'Trust me,' he implores. 'You can read my mind. So go ahead, read it. See what kind of man I am.'

The fake Doctor hesitates, looking the real Doctor in the eyes.

'I promise you, I will not let the Sycorax hurt you,' the Doctor assures his doppelgänger.

The second Doctor nods and throws his arms wide. There is a burst of intense white light, then a stream of gold dust seems to shoot from his fingers. For a long moment he stands there like a human roman candle and then the light fades and when it does, the fake Doctor is no longer there. Instead you see a small hairless grey creature that looks a bit like a baby elephant. It is weak and falls to the ground, unconscious.

Suddenly there is a mighty roar from behind you and the red-robed Sycorax leader appears, brandishing a pair of sharp swords. He runs at the helpless creature intent on harm, but you stick out a foot and the alien goes flying.

He gets to his feet, recovering one of the swords, but the Doctor has picked up the other one.

A frantic sword fight begins. At first the Doctor seems to be holding his own but the bony alien is strong and fast and soon begins to fight back, pushing the Doctor into a rocky alcove with no hope of escape.

With a final swish of his right arm, the Sycorax disarms the Doctor, sending his sword flying through the air. 'Doctor!' screams Amy.

The Doctor is helpless, but then the energy creature stirs and hesitantly raises one of its thick-set paws. A tiny orange blob of energy sparkles around the paw and, with his last act, the creature fires it at the Sycorax who is instantly vaporised.

Amy and you hurry to help the Doctor, but he is more interested in checking out the energy creature. He shakes his head sadly – the creature has died.

If you go to the Doctor, go to 65.

If Amy goes to the Doctor, go to 76.

DOCTOR WHO

Also Available:

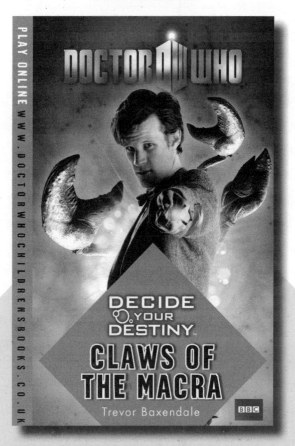

PLAY ONLINE WWW.DOCTORWHOCHILDRENSBOOKS.CO.UK

DOCTOR WHO

DECIDE YOUR DESTINY

CLAWS OF THE MACRA

Trevor Baxendale

BBC

ISBN: 978-1-40590-685-2